GUARDIAN *of the* HILLS

GUARDIAN *of the* HILLS

Victoria Strauss

Morrow Junior Books
New York

Printed in the United States of America.

1 2 3 4 5 6 7 8 9 10

Library of Congress Cataloging-in-Publication Data
Strauss, Victoria.
Guardian of the hills / Victoria Strauss.
p. cm.
Summary: The evil spirit of Stern Dreamer sleeps for centuries
until archaeologists uncover his ancient tomb; now only his
direct descendant Pamela, who has lived apart from her
Native American heritage, can imprison his spirit again.
ISBN 0-688-06998-3
1. Indians of North America—Juvenile fiction. [1. Indians of North America—
Fiction. 2. Archaeology—Fiction. 3. Supernatural—Fiction.] I. Title.
PZ7.S9125Ke 1995
[Fic]—dc20 95-1771 CIP AC

Prologue

Pamela pushed through the screen door, letting it fall closed behind her with a crash and a twang of springs. The still, hot air of the afternoon swallowed up the sound. She made her way across the back veranda, down the long flight of stairs, and into the yard. Before her lay the tangled expanse of the garden. At the garden's foot the forest began, a screen of rough-barked trunks and trembling leaves. Only the smallest gap marked the path to the hills.

Pamela had arrived home that morning. Patiently she had endured the greeting, gossiping, and unpacking that always accompanied her returns; dutifully she had eaten a large lunch that included most of her favorite foods. All the while she had been aware of the need to leave the house and seek the woods. As always, she disciplined herself to ignore it, pushing it to the back of her mind until the rituals of return were satisfied. Every arrival after a long absence was the same. Except perhaps for this one. This time, she had come home for good.

At last Pamela was free to answer the call that drew her down the garden path, between the beds of vegetables and flowers, and into the woods. With the first step beneath the trees, she moved from summer's merciless glare into a cool green shadowland. On careful feet she followed the path, marking the small things that had changed during her absence: a fallen tree, a sapling grown taller, a new stand of flowers. She passed the Indian settlement, its houses shuttered and quiet in the shimmering afternoon, and the little track that led to Mirabel's cabin. A few more steps brought her to the edge of the valley.

She paused just inside the final fringe of trees. The valley lay before her, brimming with sunlight, a grassy bowl holding at its center five strange flat hills. She felt the familiar mixture of emotions this place elicited—recognition, pain, wonder—shot through, as always, with the darker thread of fear, and a reluctance to step away from the safe shadows beneath the trees. Instinctively her eyes searched the slopes for the sooty shapes of crows.

But there were no crows here now, she reminded herself. This was her home; she belonged here more than anywhere else in the world. The fear was only a part of that, a necessary part, keeping her always mindful of what this sleepy place contained.

Pamela stepped out into the sun. She jogged down the uneven slope toward the largest, central hill. The heat poured down on her unprotected head and arms; sweat beaded on her cheeks and forehead.

Reaching the flat expanse of the hilltop, Pamela paced slowly around all four sides. The short grass was like the pelt of an animal, sleek and without blemish. There was no sign that it had ever been disturbed.

Pamela sat down cross-legged in the middle of the hill. It was very quiet; not a breeze stirred to ease the weight of the sun. Pamela closed her eyes, putting both hands palm-down on the springy turf. She felt the tug of the past, as irresistible as the heat. She surrendered to it, allowing her mind to arrow backward, back through more than ten years of experience and change, to the winter of her sixteenth year.

Chapter ONE

Outside the windows of the train, the unfamiliar woodland rushed past. The trees were bare, the ground muffled under a brown shroud of fallen leaves. Here and there houses appeared briefly between the trunks, bringing swift impressions of slatted walls, blank windows, empty yards.

Pamela sat with her cheek against the glass, numb with change and lack of sleep. She felt as if she had passed right out of the known world during the long night. More than twenty-four hours ago they had left the familiar Connecticut landscape behind, moving south, then turning west in Virginia to begin the long trek across the inland states. Night fell in Richmond. Morning brought Memphis: a brief stopover and a hasty meal. A new train took them through the outskirts of the city, past a vast hobo camp, across the great expanse of the Mississippi. The train was moving into Arkansas now, on the last leg of the journey. In a little more than two hours they would reach their destination.

Pamela looked to her mother, dozing in the seat opposite. A crease came and went between Elizabeth's penciled brows; there were marks like bruises beneath her eyes. Yet not even travel and exhaustion could mar her beauty. Her skin was a warm brown, her eyes long and tilted and nearly black, her nose slightly flattened over the nostrils, her cheekbones high and broad. Her heavy hair was jet black; it would not hold a permanent wave, and she wore it unfashionably, coiled into a bun at the back of her neck. It was difficult to believe she was no more than half-Indian. Her European ancestry showed only in the chiseling of her lips and a creaminess beneath her dark complexion. Pamela often wished she looked like her mother. Yet it had always been a source of pride to Elizabeth that Pamela looked so un-Indian, with her reddish brown hair, regular features, hazel eyes, and pale skin as fair and fine as her father's.

Pamela turned her attention back to the alien landscape, thinking about what lay ahead: an Arkansas town called Flat Hills, a house where her mother had grown up, and her grandfather. Pamela knew that her grandfather was a lawyer, that his wife had been a full-blooded Quapaw Indian who had died when Pamela's mother was still a child, and that he lived in the big house that had belonged to his family since pioneer days. But that was all. In her entire life Pamela had never met her grandfather.

Pamela had wondered about this occasionally when she was young, about the source of the deep division between her mother and grandfather. All Elizabeth ever said, when pushed, was that Arkansas was much too far away to visit. Only the formal greeting cards, which never failed to arrive at Christmas and on Elizabeth's birthday, broke the enduring silence between father and daughter.

But then the Great Depression came, like a cold wind across the country. Banks closed, businesses collapsed, jobs failed. Pamela's closest friend and her family lost their house to foreclosure. Hoboes drifted through town, sleeping in the rail yard; long lines formed every day at the soup kitchen. Every night the radio brought news of unemployment, hunger, and despair.

Pamela's father had died some years before, leaving them well provided for; Elizabeth had supplemented the income from his wise investments with a successful flower-arranging business. But the Depression swallowed the investments and left little demand for luxuries such as flowers. Piece by piece, Elizabeth began to sell off the property Pamela's father had purchased over the years. It brought in money, enough to live on if they were careful. But one day Pamela returned home from school to find Elizabeth sitting by the window, staring blankly out at the winter landscape. Her shoulders were slumped and her hands lay limp in her lap. She turned her face to her daughter.

"The land's gone," she said. "I sold the last of it today. There's nothing left now, except the house."

Pamela stared at her mother. She had never seen Elizabeth look so defeated.

"I don't know what to do, Pamela," Elizabeth said, and the hopelessness in her voice was the most terrible thing Pamela had ever heard. "I just don't know what we're going to do."

That night after supper, Elizabeth sat Pamela down in the front room and took both her daughter's hands in hers. Her face was determined: Pamela knew a decision had been made.

"Pamela," Elizabeth said. "You know how hard things have been for us. My flower business is barely surviving, and there aren't any jobs to be had—once the money from this last land sale is gone, there won't be enough coming in to live on. We're two months behind on the mortgage as it is, and the bank is threatening to foreclose. I've thought and thought about what to do, and there's only one thing I can see." She took a deep breath. "We have to go to my father in Arkansas."

Pamela stared at her mother, speechless. It was as if Elizabeth had told her they were going to the moon. Elizabeth tightened her grip on her daughter's hands.

"I know this is sudden, darling. I know it'll be hard for you to leave your school and your friends. But I just can't see any other way for us. Your grandfather is a rich man. He can give you opportunities I can't possibly provide. It's for the best, really it is. Can you understand that? Can you try?"

"I . . . I guess so," Pamela managed through dry lips.

"It won't be so bad, you'll see. Flat Hills is . . . it's actually quite a nice town. There's a movie theater, and an ice-cream parlor. The house is big—you'll have your own room, just the way you do here. You'll make friends in school. You'll come to like it. I'm sure you will."

The next weeks were a whirlwind of activity. Elizabeth arranged for their home to be put on the market, and for its contents to be sold for cash. They would be taking with them only what could fit into their trunks and suitcases. Daily the house became emptier. Pamela felt as if her life were being wiped away. Questions struggled within her; why Arkansas, after all these years of silence? Was there really no alternative but to leave their entire life behind, no option but to go live with someone Pamela had never met, someone with whom Elizabeth had barely communicated for longer than Pamela could remember? But Elizabeth's frenetic activity was like a barrier. Behind it she seemed to have grown very distant.

And so Pamela did not ask questions. She did not shout, as she sometimes wished she could, that it was unfair, that she did not want to go, that she knew she would hate strange, faraway Arkansas, where she had no friends and nothing would be familiar. Instead she watched silently as the underpinnings of her world disappeared. The floor seemed to tremble beneath her feet sometimes, as if she stood at the edge of an abyss. At its bottom waited a blank called Flat Hills, a shadow called her grandfather, and a new life she did not want and could not even imagine.

Pamela woke to a hand on her arm. "Sit up, Pamela," her mother said. "We're almost there."

Pamela obeyed. Uneasy dreams had flashed through her sleep, dark and tangled like the passing forests. Her legs and back ached from the hardness of the seats.

Elizabeth began to prepare herself. First she took down and combed her hair, coiling it neatly away again. Tucking a handkerchief inside the collar of her blouse, she dusted pale powder over her face and neck, pausing to let it settle, repeating the process. Rouge came next, disguising the broad cheekbones. She carefully lined and shaded her eyes to minimize their slant and, lastly, lipsticked her lips a dark red. It was an invariable ritual: She performed it quickly, deft despite the jolting of the train. Complete, she looked no less beautiful, but much less Indian. The cosmetics gave her face a slightly masklike quality, a porcelain artificiality that her bare features did not possess.

"Tidy your hair, Pamela," she said, holding out the comb.

"You look like a little savage with it tangled up like that."

Pamela obeyed. Why must Elizabeth speak to her sometimes as if she were still a child of ten? She stood up and smoothed the wrinkles from her wool jumper, pulled up her socks, checked the knots on her plain brown oxfords, and adjusted her blouse. Stiffly she sat down once more.

The countryside had changed. The woods were now interspersed with fields and farms. Soon it became apparent that they were on the outskirts of a town. The buildings were shabby and unpainted, roofed with corrugated tin or wooden shingles. The train slowed, running parallel to a paved road lined with houses and stores. At last, the wheels squealing, the train pulled into the station, halting with a final jolt and a great hissing of steam.

Elizabeth was on her feet, adjusting her hat and buttoning her coat. She wrestled their luggage down from the overhead rack, tottering slightly on her high heels. They had brought with them only two suitcases; the trunks would follow later, by freight. The stationmaster, an aged man in a neat blue uniform, took the cases, extending a hand to assist Elizabeth down the steps. Almost as their feet touched the platform the train rocked, shot up jets of steam, and groaned slowly out of the station, picking up speed as it disappeared round the bend of the tracks. The clacking of its wheels faded, lost in distance.

The stationmaster placed their cases on the platform and vanished inside the station house. Pamela looked at her mother; Elizabeth's face was calm, but she was tugging and smoothing her elegant gloves, a sign that she was nervous. There was no one else on the platform. Pamela hugged herself against the raw chill of the air.

There was the sound of footsteps: A man mounted the platform steps and approached them. Beside her, Pamela felt her mother's immobility.

"Well, Elizabeth," said the man, reaching them. His voice was soft and slightly hoarse.

"Well, Father."

Elizabeth moved forward, rested one hand lightly on his shoulder, and touched her lips briefly to his cheek. She stepped back and put an arm around Pamela's shoulders.

"This is Pamela."

Pamela looked up at him. Her grandfather, she thought. He was tall and very slightly stooped; silver hair showed beneath his hat. His deep-set eyes were overhung by bushy brows. His features were large and well defined, his skin weathered, as if he spent a good deal of time outdoors. Despite the lines on his face, he gave an impression of strength and fitness.

"Hello, Pamela," he said gravely. He glanced at Elizabeth. "She favors her father."

Pamela felt a momentary tightening of her mother's fingers. "Yes," Elizabeth answered.

He bent and lifted their suitcases and led the way across the platform to a large sleek black car parked in the street. It was a recent-model Packard, with sweeping rounded contours and polished chrome. It seemed utterly out of place on the shabby street.

There was no conversation as they drove away from the station. Pamela's grandfather stared straight ahead; Elizabeth looked out the window, her face weary. The silence felt oppressive. The town rolled past the windows of the car: The dilapidated houses gave way to a downtown area of shops and businesses, which gave way in turn to streets of well-kept dwellings with substantial lawns. The car turned at last into a driveway, and Pamela looked up at the place that was to be her home.

Chapter TWO

It was a large house, built of white-painted boards, with gingerbread trim around the eaves and the long porch, and wide green shutters on the French windows of the ground floor. The lawn, bordered by a tall hedge, was meticulously landscaped, with shrubs done up in sacking for the winter. Curtains were drawn across all the windows; the house seemed to be asleep.

The front door opened onto a wide hallway lined with bookshelves, with big double doors opening off both sides and a staircase at the back. Pamela's grandfather led the way to the upstairs hall, identical to the one below. He set the cases down.

"You'll have your old room, Elizabeth," he said. "Pamela may have the room next door."

"Thank you, Father," said Elizabeth.

"Well, I will leave you to rest. Dinner is at seven promptly."

He turned and went down the stairs. His back had a dismissive quality; it was as if he had already forgotten them.

Pamela looked at her mother, feeling dazed.

"The bathroom is at the end of the hall," Elizabeth said. "Why don't you have a bath. But be quick, because I want one too."

Pamela's room was a pleasant surprise. It was large, the walls papered in a pretty sprigged pattern of blue flowers. The bed had a dark wooden headboard and was covered with a white flocked spread. There was a sit-down dressing table with a marble top, an oval mirror, and many small drawers with oddly shaped pulls like little tassels. A big wardrobe stood beside it. Opposite the bed was a fireplace; a coal fire winked in the grate.

There were windows on either side of the bed, their blue curtains half-drawn. The windows faced the backyard, which was large and less manicured than the front. A great leafless mass of trees came right up to its rear edge. Pamela thought of the lost Connecticut woods, of the white snow-carpet that hid the browns and blacks and bronzes and transformed the winter world. Did it ever snow here? She stared out at the gray landscape dimming with the approach of evening. The floor seemed to sway slightly, as if she were still on the train.

A wash and a change of clothes made her feel somewhat better. She busied herself for a while unpacking, until sounds in the next room announced that Elizabeth had finished her own bath. She knocked at Elizabeth's door and heard her mother's soft "Come in."

Having removed her makeup in the bath, Elizabeth was now going through the entire ritual again. She had washed her hair; black and glossy, it hung over her shoulders to dry. Pamela sat down on the bed, glancing around. This was the room in which Elizabeth had spent her childhood. It was very much like Pamela's, with similar furniture and wallpaper. There were no photographs or knickknacks, no books or mementos of Elizabeth's youth, only Elizabeth's current possessions: the dress laid out on a chair, the array of cosmetics and face creams spread across the dressing table, the open suitcase.

"Mother," said Pamela at last, tentatively.

"Yes, Pamela?" Elizabeth was carefully applying lipstick and spoke through stretched lips.

"Does Grandfather not want us here?"

Elizabeth's hand stopped moving; after a second she turned around. "Of course he wants us here."

Pamela looked down at the white bedspread. "He didn't seem very glad to see us."

"It's not that, Pam. It's just . . . well, it's been a long time, for both of us. We have to get used to each other again."

Her makeup finished, Elizabeth pinned up her still-damp hair and stepped into the dress she had selected for tonight. It was a fine burgundy wool challis, cut to flatter her slim figure, with lace at the collar and cuffs. No one looking at it would guess that it had been bought years ago, when times were still good, and altered since then to keep up with changing fashion. Pamela loved and envied her mother's clothing. She longed to wear the kinds of grown-up things many of her friends at home did, but Elizabeth still chose for Pamela the same jumpers, jerseys, and pleated skirts Pamela had worn when she was ten years old. It was, Pamela sometimes thought, as if her mother wished her to remain a child forever.

"Button me up, will you, Pam?" Pamela obeyed. When she was finished, Elizabeth turned. She placed her hand against her daughter's cheek. "I know you're feeling lost and lonely just now, darling. But it'll pass, I promise. Everything will be all right. This time next year, you'll hardly even re-member Connecticut. All right, darling?"

Pamela felt her eyes filling with tears. She went into her mother's arms. But after only a moment, firmly, Elizabeth pulled away.

"Look at you, you're all mussed again," she said gently.

Deftly she smoothed Pamela's hair and clothing. She ad-justed her own dress, straightened the seams of her stockings, and stooped to peer in the mirror one last time. Then, taking a deep breath as if to prepare herself, she led the way into the hall.

The big downstairs parlor was both luxurious and coldly formal. The antique furnishings were upholstered in expen-sive-looking gold fabric, and a large Oriental rug lay on the floor. The three long windows were curtained in a rich gold brocade with white lace undercurtains, drawn now against the dark of the winter evening. Lamps were lit, and at one end of the room yet another coal fire burned in a large grate.

The dining room opened off the parlor. A big sideboard stood against one wall, displaying silver bowls, trays, and serving utensils. Against another wall was a large, glass-fronted china cabinet. The long table was covered with a white damask cloth and set for three. Pamela's grandfather was al-ready seated.

The meal was substantial: a roast of beef, a dish of pars-leyed potatoes, hot rolls, and a vegetable unpleasantly like spinach but more bitter, cooked with fat chunks of bacon. The food was served by a stout middle-aged black woman who brought the dishes in through a door that seemed to lead not to another part of the house but to the outside. Later Pamela found out that because of the heat that prevailed for much of the year, the kitchen was built apart from the house, connected to it by a long veranda at the back.

"Well, Father," said Elizabeth after they had eaten in silence for some time. "Everything looks just the same."

He glanced up. "Yes."

"I'd almost forgotten how big this house is. Usually when you go back to a place things seem small. But everything is larger than I remember."

"It's been a while."

He was looking directly at her; Elizabeth dropped her eyes to her plate. "Do you still keep up the big flower garden in back?"

"Some. Sam can't do as much as he used to."

"So Sam is still here." Elizabeth looked at Pamela. "Sam is a wonderful gardener. Wait till you see this place in the summer . . . Is Coralie still with you?"

"She died, three years back."

"Oh. What a shame."

"It was pneumonia."

"What a shame," Elizabeth repeated. "She was a wonderful cook. I still remember her peach pie."

"Esther manages tolerably well."

"Oh, yes," Elizabeth agreed. "Of course. The meal is delicious."

Silence fell. Elizabeth seemed to have run out of small talk, and her father made no attempt to fill the gap. Surreptitiously Pamela watched him. He ate with concentration, methodically clearing his plate. His hands were large and well manicured, their ropy veins and large knuckles more reflective of his age than his face. He wore a gray cardigan over his shirt and tie, but the effect was only slightly less formal than a jacket would have been. Pamela could see nothing of Elizabeth in his features.

The woman—Esther—seemed to have a special sense that let her know when they were finished; almost as the forks were laid down she appeared to carry away the main course and bring dessert, a light pudding with an orange-flavored sauce. Over it, Pamela's grandfather spoke.

"Have you everything you need, Elizabeth?"

"Yes, Father. Everything's fine."

"There are extra blankets if you want them, in the linen closet in the hall. But I'm sure you remember." Abruptly he swung his eyes toward Pamela. "And you, young lady. Are you comfortable?"

Pamela swallowed a bite of pudding a bit too fast, and coughed. When she could speak, she said: "Yes, thank you. My room is very nice."

"Good," said her grandfather, and once again the conversation died.

Dinner over, they moved into the parlor.

"Pamela, why don't you get a book for yourself?" Elizabeth suggested. "The bookshelves are in the hall."

Pamela went out into the hall. There was quite a selection of books, but most of them were dry grown-up novels; though there were a number of works for young people, all seemed to date from the first years of the century and were hopelessly old-fashioned. Perhaps they had been Elizabeth's when she was young.

Pamela picked something out more or less at random and returned to the parlor, where she seated herself in the corner of one of the sofas. Her grandfather was reading a heavy-looking volume and smoking his pipe, which filled the room with a pleasant, winey tobacco scent. Elizabeth worked on one of the needlepoint projects she always seemed to have in progress. The air sang slightly, punctuated by the ticking of the mantel clock and the occasional soft thump of coal breaking apart in the grate.

At last Elizabeth looked up. "Bedtime, Pamela," she said. "It's been a long day."

Gratefully Pamela abandoned her boring book and went over to kiss her mother on the cheek. "Good night, Mother," she said. She looked at her grandfather and hesitated. "Good night, Grandfather," she said finally, stumbling over the unfamiliar title.

He glanced up. "Good night, young lady."

Up in her room, Pamela undressed—quickly, as it was distinctly chilly. She switched off the bedside light and the room dropped into darkness, punctuated by the dull orange eye of the coal fire. She shut her mind to the black despair that threatened to overwhelm her, refusing to allow herself the luxury of pretending to be in her own lost room in Connecticut, or of sobbing into her pillow.

Much later, it seemed, she was awakened by the low sound of voices downstairs. Her mother and grandfather were talking. Drawn by irresistible curiosity, she tiptoed out onto the landing and leaned over the banister. A swath of golden light spread out onto the floor of the darkened hall below.

"Time," her grandfather was saying in his measured, slightly husky voice. "Time is the trouble, Elizabeth. So much of it has passed."

There was the sound of a sigh. "I know that, Father."

"You can't expect me to behave as if nothing had happened. In all these years you never answered any of my cards. Not a word, not a letter, not a photograph. And now here you are in my house."

"Pamela has nothing to do with that. All I'm asking you to do is to give her a chance. She's your granddaughter."

"That has never mattered to you before. You've made her a stranger to me. As you are."

"Do you think I'd be here if there'd been any other way? If it was just me, I'd never have come back. Never."

Elizabeth's words were quiet, but Pamela could not mistake the depth of feeling that infused them.

There was a pause. Then Pamela's grandfather, his voice low: "Do you hate me that much?"

"Oh, Father. You don't understand. Pamela is all that's important now. I can't provide for her by myself anymore. But you can. You can give her all the things I can't. Throw me out if you want, I don't care. But don't let whatever lies between us touch her."

"How you dramatize things, Elizabeth. This is your home. It always has been. It was your choice to leave it, not mine."

"Just give her a chance, Father. That's all I ask."

"The blood barely shows in her."

The word *blood* held a strange emphasis. It was a moment before Elizabeth replied.

"Her blood is mostly like yours, Father. I married a white man, remember?"

"I remember." There was a brief silence. "How like your mother you are, Elizabeth."

"And what's that supposed to mean?" Elizabeth's tone held a quick anger that seemed disproportionate to her father's comment.

"Exactly what the words denote." Pamela's grandfather sounded mild. "Elizabeth, if we're going to live together, we must try to get along. I am not . . . the most flexible of men. But I will make the effort, if you will."

There was a silence, and then Elizabeth spoke. She sounded very weary. "You're right, Father. I'm . . . I'm just very tired. I think I'll go up to bed now. We can start fresh in the morning."

"Yes. In the morning."

Pamela heard the staccato *click* of her mother's high heels as she crossed the parlor floor. Silently she ducked back into her room. She leaned her head against the door and closed her eyes, no longer fighting despair. Tears rolled down her cheeks; it did not seem worthwhile to suppress them. Why had they come here, to a house where they were not welcome, to a place her mother hated? Pamela missed her home. She missed her friends. She missed her old life. She loathed the terrible changes that had brought her here. The future stretched out before her, dull and gray and lonely.

After a while she went to one of the windows and drew back the curtains. The sky had cleared slightly, and the moon could be seen through ragged cloud-trails. The backyard was a pale wash of moonlight, the woods a dark and formless mass. Unbidden, her grandfather's voice came back to her. *Blood*, he had said, with that strange emphasis. The blood doesn't show in her.

Indian blood. That was what he had meant, Pamela knew. Within sight of these night-bound woods, the words took on new meaning. These Arkansas lands were Indian lands; these massed trees, Indian trees. Indians had lived here before her grandfather had been born, before this house had been built, before white settlers had come at all. They were still here, somewhere, in a village outside of town. The village Pamela's grandmother had come from.

Pamela shivered. It was cold by the window; she drew the curtains closed again and huddled into her bed, staring with wide dry eyes at the orange heart of the fire until it blurred, and she slipped into sleep.

Pamela dreamed. Part of her lay in a strange bed in a strange room, but part of her roamed the forest outside. On silent feet she padded through the winter-bare woods, skirting the brushy undergrowth, smelling the rich loamy scent of the rotting leaf-carpet that blanketed the ground. The moon shone intermittently through the trees, lighting the familiar path, the path traveled so many times before. The forest thinned and ended. She stood, just within its shadow. Before her lay a large yard and a great white house, its windows dark, its people sleeping. She gazed up, her eyes luminous with the moon.

In Pamela's dream, the sleeping part of herself had risen to stand by the window. The curtain was drawn away from the cold glass, and she could see across the yard and into the trees. Two round orange points of light hovered there, the eyes of a great wild beast. It had come to mark her arrival. She was filled with a sense of purpose, with a rising fear. . . .

The dream was becoming a nightmare. Uneasily Pamela stirred, half-waking, pushing it away. She fell once more into sleep, and this time her sleep was dreamless.

Chapter *THREE*

Pamela gathered up her books and joined the horde of students heading homeward for the day. All around her, classmates laughed and chattered, calling back and forth. Yet amid the hubbub, Pamela walked alone.

Even now, almost two months since she had begun attending school, Pamela had not found a place for herself. She knew the girls and boys in her class and had made some casual acquaintances. But in spite of every effort, she had not acquired any real friends, or become part of any group.

She had done her best. She initiated conversations, she joined the chorus and the Library Club, she attended pep rallies and basketball games, she smiled and was pleasant and made herself available for friendship. Yet friendship did not come. Occasionally, when she volunteered a comment in class or made a suggestion at club meetings, she was met with outright hostility. Elizabeth, when asked, explained that Southerners distrusted Northerners. It would take time for people to forget Pamela was from Connecticut. But Pamela was dubious. It was difficult to imagine that just coming from another part of the country could be enough to make others dislike her.

Of all the terrible things about Flat Hills, this was the worst. Never before had Pamela been an outcast. Never before had she lacked friends, activities, acceptance. Never before had she belonged nowhere, as she did now.

Pamela descended the great flight of steps at the front of the high school, and crossed the lawn. March had brought spring to Arkansas. Cherry trees bloomed along the streets, sugar pink clouds of blossom. Beneath them, the new grass was already long enough for mowing.

"What a lovely outfit," someone said.

Pamela stopped, startled. It was Dolores Folsom who had spoken. Dolores was a tall blond girl with a curving mouth that seemed always to be laughing, usually at someone else. She was the leader of an influential clique. She was looking at Pamela now, smiling; behind her clustered the girls of her group.

Pamela knew very well that no one who was wearing a grown-up print dress and lipstick could possibly admire her own plain, pleated skirt, round-collared white blouse, and flat lace-up shoes. She wished she could ignore Dolores or say something cutting, but it was best to avoid trouble. She smiled briefly and tried to walk on. Dolores moved in front of her, forcing her to stop.

"It looks new. *Brand* new."

"It's not new," Pamela said. "It's years old."

Dolores smiled slyly. "Well, now that I really look, I can see you must've had those clothes a while. Since grade school, at least."

The other girls giggled. Pamela felt herself flush. Stepping around Dolores, she began to walk away. She had gone no more than a few steps when someone's voice floated after her.

"Go home, papoose. Run on home to mother!"

Pamela felt her shame transform abruptly into anger. She turned around and marched back.

"Who said that?" she demanded.

Dolores and the others were silent. They looked at her, their eyes intent.

"What did I ever do to you?" Pamela fought to keep her voice steady. "What is it that makes you so nasty to me?"

Dolores's smile was mean. "You don't belong here."

"I have as much right here as anyone!"

"No, you don't. All the other Indians go to the colored school. That's where you should be. Not in *our* school."

It was a moment before Pamela could speak. "But I'm only a quarter Indian!"

"That's the part that counts around here."

"That's . . . that's just stupid!"

"Listen, papoose." Dolores was no longer smiling. "You're the one who's stupid. Don't you know you're only in our school because your grandfather is the richest man in town and thinks he can order people around? But just because everyone kowtows to him doesn't mean we have to treat you the same. We know where you belong, even if you don't."

The other girls were silent, their faces predatory. They were waiting for Pamela to cry. She defied them. She lifted her chin and walked away from them as fast as she could. After a moment their laughter followed her, and their voices:

"Run home to mother, papoose! Run home to the Indian squaw! Run home to the reservation!"

Pamela turned the corner at last. Safely out of view, she gave in to tears of humiliation and pain. In all her life no one had ever spoken to her the way Dolores just had, with such hostility, such . . . contempt. Was that the real reason she had not been able to find a place here? Because she was part Indian? No one had ever cared about it before.

Until now, Pamela had never thought to notice that there were no Indians at her school. In fact, she had never seen an Indian in Flat Hills at all. Dolores's comment about the colored school returned hatefully to her mind. Flat Hills was full of signs that said things like COLORED ENTRANCE, COLORED DRINKING FOUNTAIN, COLORED REST ROOMS, and WE DO NOT SERVE NEGROES. This had shocked Pamela—she had been taught by her parents that everyone, black or white, was deserving of respect—but it would never have occurred to her that Indians were included in these prohibitions. No one had ever refused to serve Pamela in a store or told her not to enter through the door reserved for whites. Could this really be only because of her grandfather? Perhaps that was why her mother hated Flat Hills, why she never went out, why she had taken to spending all day in her room.

Pamela felt another wave of misery. How would it be possible to live here, to go to school every day, knowing that people were looking at her and thinking she did not belong? How could she hold her head up and meet people's eyes, knowing that they hated her for something that was not her fault? It was not fair. She was hardly Indian at all. She didn't look Indian, she didn't act Indian, she knew almost nothing about Indians. How could such a little part of her transform the rest into something others hated?

Pamela had reached the house by this time. Slowly she mounted the stairs to her room. She paused outside her mother's door. After a moment's hesitation, she raised her hand and knocked. Elizabeth's soft voice told her to enter.

Elizabeth was sitting in a chair by the window, reading a book. The curtains were half-drawn, and the room was wrapped in the dimness that gripped the rest of the house. As always, Elizabeth was impeccably dressed and made up, even in the privacy of her room where no one could see her. She looked up and smiled.

"Hello, darling. How was school?"

Pamela sat down on the bed, putting her books by her side. She folded her hands tightly together. "That's what I want to talk to you about."

Taking a deep breath, she told her story. When she had finished, there was a silence. Elizabeth had dropped her eyes as Pamela spoke, regarding her hands, folded on her upturned book. Her face looked, suddenly, very tired.

"I'm sorry you had to hear that," she said at last. "I guess things here haven't changed."

Pamela had to struggle to keep frustration out of her voice. "Why didn't you tell me? Why did you let me find out all by myself?"

"Oh, darling." Elizabeth sighed. "I thought . . . I thought if I told you, you'd be frightened and unhappy. It was hard enough for you coming here, I didn't want to put that burden on you too. I hoped, I really hoped, that things had changed."

"But you must have known what was happening when I told you I wasn't fitting in."

"Pamela, I did what I thought was best. I was only thinking of you. Of what's best for you. You have to let me be the judge of that, darling."

Pamela believed her mother, yet it was always the same: Why must Elizabeth treat her as if she must be protected from the truth? "Mother, *why* do they hate Indians?" she persisted.

"It's not easy to explain, Pamela. People hate . . . what's different from them. If something is just a little different, or there's just a little of it, it's seen as exotic and interesting, but if there's a lot of difference, a lot of people who live differently and think differently and believe differently, that's when hatred happens. The Indians . . . the Indians don't want to change—they don't want to be like other people. They keep their own language. They have different beliefs, superstitions, traditions. . . ." Elizabeth's voice trailed off. Her eyes dropped to the book on her lap.

"What kind of traditions, Mother?"

"I just don't know that much about it, Pamela."

"But your mother was an Indian. A full-blooded Indian. Didn't she tell you?"

Elizabeth looked up, then away. "No. It was part of her bargain with my father."

"A bargain?"

"My mother was brought up in the Indian village. But she wanted to better herself. She wanted to go to college. She got a job as a maid so she could save money. But she met my father. She married him instead." Elizabeth paused and shook her head.

"You have to understand, Pamela, what a thing it was for my father to marry my mother. The prejudice then was even worse than it is now. My father comes from one of the oldest families in this county, but even so, most people in town wouldn't have anything to do with him after the marriage. My father had to practice law in another town, where they didn't know he had an Indian wife. My mother had to travel miles to do her shopping. It was incredibly hard, for both of them.

"Before they got married, they made a bargain. My father promised my mother that he would never leave Flat Hills, and my mother promised my father that she would put her Indian ways aside. And she did. You would never have known she came from the Indian village at all. The only thing she ever told me was that she had been brought up to very different beliefs, very different traditions, but those weren't for me, because I was my father's daughter."

For just an instant, an undercurrent of bitterness touched Elizabeth's voice.

"But my father tried to break the bargain. He wanted to find a place where they could live and not be so weighed down by prejudice. My mother refused. He could never understand why. They quarreled about it—terrible quarrels. I used to hear them at night, after I'd gone to bed. They fought and fought—but eventually they stopped fighting. He stopped speaking to her. They lived in the house like two strangers. My mother could bear anything, but not his silence. She was like a ghost. She stopped going outside, she sat in her room all day doing nothing."

Silence fell. Elizabeth's face was dark, shadowed with memory. Pamela heard the faint hiss as coal burned in the grate. She willed her mother to go on, to finish the story. She had never heard Elizabeth say so much about her family before. But the silence stretched out, and still Elizabeth did not speak. At last, softly, Pamela said:

"What happened?"

"My mother died. Gradually people began to forgive my father for marrying an Indian woman, even to forget about it. Though there was always me to remind them."

"You didn't go to the colored school, did you?"

Elizabeth looked horrified. "Certainly not. Where did you get such an idea?"

"Dolores said that the other Indian children go to the colored school." Pamela swallowed. "That . . . that I should be there too."

"The Indian children who go to the black school are from the village." Elizabeth's voice was angry. "They have no family, they have no money, they have nothing. You're from one of the oldest families in town. Of course you go to the white school. There's no question of anything else. You mustn't pay attention to what people like Dolores say. They're ignorant. Just ignorant."

"Did you ever make any friends?"

"Of course I had friends. Pamela, darling, not everyone in this town hates Indians. You'll make friends, you'll see. You'll find some nice girl who's nothing like Dolores."

Elizabeth was using that tone again, that soothing, talking-to-a-child tone.

"How can you say that, Mother, after what you just told me? They hate me. They *hate* me! All because of something I never asked for, something I don't even care about! Maybe I should go find the other Indians. They'd be my friends.

They wouldn't hate me for being part white."

"That's out of the question." Elizabeth's voice snapped like a whip. "I won't have you going anywhere near the Indians. Not ever."

Pamela stared at her mother, startled. "But why?"

"If you think the prejudice is bad now, it's nothing to how it would be if you associated with Indian children! The only way to beat the Doloreses of this world is to prove them wrong. Even if they never see their mistakes, others will. That's how you become accepted. Not by embracing what others hate in you! Not by doing what they expect!"

Elizabeth's voice was harsh. Pamela blinked, fighting tears, knowing how much her mother hated it when she cried.

"Anyway," Elizabeth said more gently, "you have no idea how the Indians live. They have nothing, no modern conveniences, no heat, no running water, no electricity. They're poorer than the poorest whites and blacks in this town. They live as they lived hundreds of years ago—it's primitive. Some of them don't speak English. A lot of the children don't go to school. There are epidemics of disease—scarlet fever, diphtheria, typhoid. And all because they would rather hold on to beliefs that are thousands of years old than change and become part of the modern world."

For a moment Elizabeth's face was faraway again; then, firmly, she shook her head, as if pushing her thoughts away.

"Don't you have homework to do, darling?"

Pamela recognized dismissal. Obediently she picked up her books and got to her feet. She crossed the room and kissed her mother's cheek. Elizabeth was already returning to her book. "I'll see you at supper, Pam darling," she said, not looking up.

In Pamela's own room the curtains, as usual, had been half-drawn by Esther. Pamela put her books down on her dressing table and opened her windows wide to the soft light and air of the spring afternoon. She propped her pillows up against the headboard of the bed and sat down to think.

In one half hour, she had found out more about her mother's life than she had been able to glean in the past sixteen years. It was a sketch, the outline of a story only, but it was not hard to fill the gaps Elizabeth had left. Pamela thought of her mother's childhood—the taunts, the separateness, the loneliness. She thought of her grandfather and grandmother—they must have loved each other very much to defy the prejudice of Flat Hills, but still they were torn apart by that very prejudice. She imagined Elizabeth, listening in the dark to their bitter quarrels. Perhaps Elizabeth blamed her father for her mother's unhappiness. Perhaps that was the source of the division between them.

And then Elizabeth had met and married Pamela's father and moved to Connecticut. How wonderful it must have been to escape, to find a life in which no one cared about her Indian heritage. She must have wanted to forget Flat Hills entirely, leave it behind as if it had never been. And so Elizabeth never spoke of her Indianness or her childhood. She never communicated with her father.

But Pamela's father had died, the Depression had come, things had fallen apart. Elizabeth was forced to return to the place where she had been so unhappy. Pamela thought of the conversation she had overheard that first night in Flat Hills, of the bitterness in her mother's voice. And in her grand-father's . . .

Pamela got up from her bed and went to stand at the window. The afternoon was beginning to fade, and the thick mass of trees at the foot of the garden bulked dark against the pale sky. Why was she here? she thought for the thousandth time. She could not find it in herself to accept that there had been no choice other than Flat Hills. Why had they not gone somewhere else, anywhere at all, a place where being part Indian made no difference?

Tomorrow she must return to school. With a wave of misery, Pamela imagined Dolores's blue eyes, the soft sound of her laughter. Existence had been bleak before, but while Pamela did not know the source of her exclusion, there had at least been the hope that it might end. Now there was no hope at all. She was part Indian; she would always be part Indian. Nothing she could do would ever change that.

What were they like, these Indians, who lived somewhere outside of Flat Hills in the poverty Elizabeth had described, who spoke a different language, lived by different traditions, held different beliefs? Her grandmother had been one of these people. Despite the hatred, she had refused to leave Flat Hills behind.

Pamela stood for a long time staring out into the garden, while the sky grayed with twilight and the air grew chill. Only when it was completely dark did she close the window, turn on her light, and begin her homework. Around her the house was silent; she might have been the only person in it. It was an eerie, lonely feeling, and she was glad when at last the bell rang for supper.

Chapter FOUR

Pamela returned to school. The routine of classes and activities dragged on unchanged. Things were really no worse than they had been. Yet in every casual glance, every turned back, Pamela could now read the reality of her exclusion.

They hated her—very well, she would hate them back. Pamela began to meet hostile stares with eyes equally cold. She ignored even the people who had shown themselves willing to talk to her; most of them were outcasts anyway, like herself. Because she knew Dolores and the others wanted her to, she refused to quit chorus and Library Club. She did, however, stop going to basketball games, pep rallies, and assemblies. There was no point, after all. Why attend a social gathering when no one would socialize?

As March moved toward April, azaleas bloomed, and rhododendrons and iris. Apple trees spread canopies of white, their fragrance faint and heavenly. The days were long and balmy, the nights agreeably cool.

At home Pamela was as solitary as she was at school. Her grandfather was always at his law office during the day, or in court, or making the rounds of his many properties, on which he personally oversaw all maintenance and rent collection. Elizabeth either read in her room or busied herself around the house. Pamela spent the weekday afternoons doing homework, descending at six o'clock to help Esther set the table and make final preparations for supper. Supper was usually a silent affair. The rest of the evening was spent in the parlor; Pamela's grandfather read his book and smoked his pipe, Elizabeth worked at her needlepoint, and Pamela read or listened to the radio.

Saturdays were not much different. Pamela might not see her mother between breakfast and supper; for her grandfather, Saturday was a workday like any other. Sunday brought church, followed by a heavy meal, after which her grandfather napped and her mother returned to her room. By Sunday afternoon Pamela found herself almost looking forward to school as a break in the monotony.

Out of boredom Pamela sought out household chores, assisting Esther with the shopping and meal preparation and even sometimes with housework, or helping in the garden with Sam. Sam was slow and kindly, a man who spoke little to people but communicated perfectly with the plants he raised; Esther was cheerful and motherly, sympathetic to Pamela's loneliness. Neither harbored prejudices against Pamela's Indianness. She felt more comfortable with them than with her peers at school.

It was Esther who told Pamela the story of her grandfather's family. They had come to Arkansas with the first settlers and made a fortune in mining and farming. Pamela's grandfather, an only child, inherited stocks and investments, as well as a great deal of property and a position on the town council.

"He's a good man, your grandfather," Esther said. "He looks out for me and Sam. He got our money out of the banks before the Depression hit, so we didn't lose a cent. He's good to other folks too. The people who rent from him, he doesn't charge them interest if they can't pay—he even lowered rents for some, or let them stay a while for free. There'd be a lot of people sleeping on the streets if it wasn't for your grandfather. Of course," she continued darkly, "there's some ignorant folks still hold the past against him. Mostly no one cares anymore, but there's always some who just can't let it go. There's a lot of hatred round here, Miss Pamela. I expect you know that already."

But Sam and Esther, kind as they were, were no substitutes for friends Pamela's own age. She had maintained correspondence with friends in Connecticut, and she received letters from them often; but letters, eagerly anticipated and avidly read, provided only a poor shadow of the company she craved. They reminded her painfully of how far away she was from her old life. She found it harder and harder to compose letters in reply. What she really wanted was to pour her heart out, to tell the truth about how awful things were in Flat Hills. But she could not bring herself to do it; it was humiliating. More than that, something told her that her friends would not understand.

One warm Saturday in early April, Pamela was drawn to the open veranda door. She went through the screen, letting it fall closed behind her with a crash. She leaned her elbows on the veranda railing and stared down into the backyard.

The back was quite unlike the manicured front. There were several fruit trees and two tall slender pecan trees, one with a circular bench built around its base. The greater part of the yard was given to large beds of flowers and vegetables. Sam had told Pamela the yard had once been bigger, the garden beds neatly confined, but now the flowers spread out beyond their designated spaces, and the woods gained ground every year. Sam waged fierce battles with weeds, saplings, and tough Johnsongrass, but each new season forced the cession of a few more inches to the forest's slow green tide.

The day was brilliant with sun, almost hot. On such a day in Connecticut, thought Pamela, she would be outside with her friends. With her whole heart she longed to be somewhere else, anywhere but here. . . .

She stared at the trees at the bottom of the garden. A path trailed down the side of the yard, disappearing into the woods. They looked dark and tangled, as if they might swallow a person up forever. Pamela glanced back at the door into the dining room and thought of the dim, empty house. She did not want to go back inside. She walked slowly along the veranda and down the stairs, listening to the creak of the boards beneath her feet. She wandered over the grass, the sun like heavy syrup on her arms and shoulders. As she neared them, the woods did not seem so very forbidding after all. The trees were well spaced, and light sifted through the leaves.

Without making a conscious decision, Pamela moved into their shade. It was cooler here and slightly damp. After a moment she stopped and looked back: The trees had closed in behind her. She could see the path leading back toward her starting point, but the house and garden had disappeared.

In spots the woods were thick, choked with bushes and creepers and thorny vines. The hum of insects wove itself through the patterns of light and shadow. Pamela discovered that if she touched a tree its singers quieted, taking up their song again as she moved away.

The woods were honeycombed with paths, some broad and distinct, some no more than faint traces. Pamela kept to the one she had chosen, aware of the danger of becoming lost. It was difficult to fix on distinctive features amid the profusion of growth: The forest spread out without a break, thicker in some places, more open in others, but everywhere composed of the same leaves and branches and earth and stippled sun, a textured fabric of green and brown.

The trees thinned, and abruptly Pamela found herself at the top of a little cliff, which dropped to a cleared area below. She halted, wondering at this small habitation in the midst of nowhere. It held about twenty houses, built of unpainted splintery boards. They had roofs of corrugated metal or uneven wooden shingles, patched here and there with other materials, and were raised a few feet off the ground on wooden posts. Rickety porches ran across their fronts. Most had chicken coops attached, with a few chickens scratching in the dirt. A large pig moved meditatively between the houses, stopping now and then to root about amid the dust. Here and there were little garden plots, fenced in and planted haphazardly with small plants. Thin spirals of smoke rose from tin-pipe chimneys.

There was the crash of a screen door. A man emerged onto one of the porches. He slouched down in a crude wooden rocking chair and tilted his hat over his eyes. His skin was coppery brown, his hair black and startlingly long, just brushing his shoulders.

Pamela moved back into the shelter of the trees. This was the Indian village, she thought. She peered down at the ramshackle houses, more like lean-tos or outhouses than real homes, at the casual animals loose in the dirt, at the way everything seemed to sag, just on the verge of falling apart. It was exactly as her mother had described.

There was the sound of running feet and laughter. A group of children came into view, pelting along a dirt path that led away from the clearing. They dashed between the houses, calling to one another in voices distorted by distance, playing some sort of game. The words they shouted did not sound like English. They were barefoot and their clothing was ragged. The man on the porch roused himself, waving his arm and shouting something. Shrieking with laughter, the children scattered back the way they had come. The man resumed his interrupted nap. Silence settled again over the clearing. Only the muted throb of the insect-song broke the hush; nothing moved but the scratching chickens and the slight shimmer of heat rising from the metal roofs.

Pamela walked slowly onward, following the path along the crest of the hill. The forest closed around her once more. She was sobered by what she had seen. Her grandmother had grown up here, she thought; under other circumstances, Elizabeth might have lived here also. She herself might have been born here. . . .

Pamela became aware that the woods had ended. She had come to the crest of a hill overlooking a great bowl-shaped valley. At its central, lowest point, the valley cupped five very odd-looking hills. There was one large, central hill, set about with four smaller ones; all poked unnaturally out of the ground as if a giant hand had placed them there. Their tops were perfectly flat. The silver green grass that tangled their slopes could not disguise the strange regularity of their shape, suggestive of truncated pyramids.

Pamela felt a stirring of interest. Surely this was not a natural formation—though if not, she was at a loss to think what else it might be. She began to descend into the valley, the sleepy song of the crickets falling away behind her. It was farther than it looked and offered tough going: The remains of last year's vegetation were matted in tussocks beneath the new growth, and there were many stones and hidden brambles. As she progressed, the hills lost some of the geometry that distance had lent them, and she could see that they were textured by water erosion, their sloping planes bumpy and uneven. She skirted the smaller hills and approached the largest, central one. One side seemed to extend outward; it was less steep, almost like a ramp.

Accepting the challenge, Pamela began to trudge upward. The hill had not looked so very tall from far away, but soon she was panting and running with sweat. She stopped and looked up. What was the point of climbing it, after all? But an odd stubbornness would not let her give in.

She reached the top, emerging on it abruptly, like the landing at the top of a flight of stairs. It had been worth the climb. She could see the entire valley. From this vantage it looked more than ever like a great grassy bowl. The trees were a solid mass ringing its rim; the springy grass, pressed down by her feet, had already risen up to obscure signs of her passage. The air was very still.

From this height the pyramidal shape of the smaller hills

was very evident. They flanked the central hill with symmetrical precision. It was impossible that this formation had occurred naturally. Somehow, these hills had been deliberately created. But why? And by whom? Pamela felt a sense of excitement. It seemed tremendously mysterious. There was an oldness about this place, not entirely accounted for by the evident signs of the passage of time.

She walked to the middle of the hill and sat down. The heat of the sun was intense. The silence was peculiar, dead, as if someone had stopped up her ears. Pamela was tired: She could not remember the last time she had walked so far. She stretched out on her back, hooking one arm across her face to shield it from the sun.

Pamela dozed, and dozing, dreamed.

She was in a large place, a vast flat area like the hilltop. A massive building rose at one end. It was night: Torches burned on posts stuck into the ground, forming an avenue of light that led from where she stood to the foot of the great structure. Someone was approaching along the avenue, a man whose face was hidden by a strange beaked mask. Pamela did not know this person, but she had the impression that he knew her. A gold band on his left arm caught the light. He stopped, regarding her through the mask. Pamela felt something, a power, a reaching—

With a start she opened her eyes. She could not have been asleep for more than a few moments; the angle of the sun was unchanged. She felt that something had waked her, but she could see or hear nothing unusual. She sat up. The sun poured over her head and shoulders. The short grass shimmered, the air was opalescent; the whole world was unnaturally bright, excessively still, suspended in the glowing amber of the heat. Pamela turned her head, and something flashed.

It was an irregular lump of rock, lying a little distance away, strewn with glittering confetti-like flakes of mica. Pamela tilted her head this way and that, and brilliance rippled across the surface of the rock. She closed her eyes against it, and still the flecks danced across her vision, vivid against a dark background.

Chapter FIVE

Much later Pamela opened her eyes. She had fallen asleep again without realizing it, lying uncomfortably on her side with one arm under her. The sun had sunk quite a distance toward the horizon. She felt a sudden alarm: It must be very late.

There was something hard against her palm. Looking down she saw that she held the piece of rock, its mica flakes still glittering in the waning sunlight. She felt a peculiar jolt of unreality. She thought she had dreamed the rock, along with the masked man and the torches.

The rock was roughly square, about eight inches across. It was incised, with pieces of the design running off its edges, as if it had once been part of something larger. Pamela squinted at the curving lines, trying to interpret them. They seemed to come clear all at once, and she realized that they represented birds: a line of birds with sharp beaks, marching across the surface of the stone.

This was very strange. Where had the rock come from? She could have sworn she had not seen it before she lay down to sleep. Nor did she recall picking it up. She tilted it, the mica stabbing at her eyes. It was very, very old; she knew this instinctively, with the same sense that told her of the oldness of the hills. It, and they, came from a time that had nothing to do with her own.

Pamela felt as if an invisible hand had brushed her spine. The light had changed with the approach of evening, deepening to gold, laying an ocher tint across the grass. The air was weighted, electric. It felt as if a storm was coming. The ground beneath Pamela's body seemed to vibrate.

Pamela got to her feet. Quickly she descended the hill, sliding and stumbling in her haste. The lengthening shadows of the smaller hills seemed to catch at her feet; she was almost running as she passed them. Panting, she mounted the slope of the valley, looking for the break in the trees that marked the path by which she had come. Gratefully she plunged into the woods.

Some distance down the path she had to stop for breath, one hand pressed against the stitch in her side. A gust of wind stirred the undergrowth. A twig snapped. The wind died, but the stirring continued. It was as if a large body were moving amid the vegetation.

Transfixed, Pamela stared around her at the endlessly replicating curtain of leaves. Each time she looked toward where she thought the sound originated, it seemed to jump elsewhere. She gasped, and began to run.

She ran until she could hear only the sound of her own feet on the path, her own body displacing the leaves and bushes. Still she fancied that the rustling followed, and clutching the stone she had found as if it were a weapon, she blundered through the woods, her breath like fire in her lungs. She burst at last through the final rank of trees and found herself in her own backyard.

Safe in the world she knew, she stopped and turned. She could hear nothing, see nothing but the dense and faceless trees. Whatever it was had gone. Perhaps it had not followed her. Perhaps it had never been there at all. Perhaps the rustling had just been the product of her imagination, fueled by her afternoon among the flat hills, or even by a slight case of sunstroke.

The thought of sunstroke brought the recollection of her lateness. Her feet dragging, she walked through the yard and mounted the steps to the veranda.

The dining room was bright with electric light, the table setting untouched. At least she had not missed supper. She paused in the parlor doorway. Elizabeth's head was bent over her needlepoint, her grandfather's over his book; as always, Pamela could feel the distance between them.

Elizabeth looked up. "Here you are, Pamela. You're very late." Her eyes narrowed. "Where on earth have you been? You're a mess. And you're sunburnt."

Pamela put her hand to her face, suddenly conscious of the heat of her skin.

"I'm sorry. I went for a walk. I lost track of the time."

"But where did you go to get into such a state? You haven't been in the woods, have you?"

Pamela nodded.

"Oh, Pamela. You're sure to have ticks and chiggers and heaven only knows what else. You'll have to have a bath before supper."

Unexpectedly Pamela's grandfather spoke.

"Those woods can be dangerous, young lady. Some people say there are still big cats out there."

His craggy face was unreadable, as always. In spite of his lack of expression, or perhaps because of it, his gaze always made Pamela uncomfortable. She could never tell what he was thinking.

"What's that in your hand?"

Pamela swallowed. "A rock. I found it." She held it out to him.

He glanced at the carving cursorily, but then his eyes stilled and Pamela sensed his interest.

"Where did you find it?"

"At the hills. The flat-topped hills; they're in a kind of valley in the woods."

"The hills?" Elizabeth's voice sounded odd. Pamela looked at her mother. Her dark eyes were fixed on the rock, as were her grandfather's. He held out his hand.

"Let me see it."

Pamela gave it to him, strangely reluctant to let it go. He turned it over and over, gazing at it, holding it up to the light so that the mica flashed.

"How did you find this?"

"It was just there, on the grass."

"And you saw no disturbance?" He looked up at her. "No piles of earth? No holes? No signs of digging?"

Pamela shook her head. "No. Nothing."

"Tell me where you found it, Pamela. The exact location."

Why were his eyes boring into her like that? "On top of the biggest hill, the one in the center. It was lying in the middle."

"This is very odd." He turned the rock in his hands. "Very odd indeed."

"Why is it odd, Grandfather?" Pamela asked. Ordinarily she would hardly have dared to question him, but her curiosity was stronger than her reticence.

"It's a relic of an earlier people," he said, "an earlier time. It should be beneath the ground, not on top of it. But you say you saw no signs of digging. And so it is odd."

"An earlier people." Pamela felt the excitement of making a connection. "The ones who built the hills?"

His eyes narrowed. "And what would make you think someone built the hills?"

"Well . . ." His steady regard made her feel too much as if she were taking a quiz in school. "They look too regular to be just ordinary hills. They're like pyramids almost, except their tops are flat. And the way they're arranged, with the big one in the middle and the small ones around it . . . well, it just looked planned, somehow. At least I thought so."

There was a pause, and then her grandfather nodded. "You're very observant, young lady. Most girls your age wouldn't have the sense to see that. You're right about the hills. They *were* built, many centuries ago, by the people who lived in that valley."

"*Centuries*," Pamela echoed, awed.

"Yes. There was a civilization in that valley once, and the hills were a center of worship and pagan religion. For years I've been trying to find some evidence to bring an archaeological team here. I've even dug there myself, but I never found anything. But now, with this"—he held up Pamela's stone—"with this, I may be able to get someone interested."

Elizabeth got to her feet abruptly and took hold of Pamela's arm.

"That's enough, Father. Pamela doesn't want to hear about archaeology. She wants a bath, and then her supper. Don't you, Pamela?"

Afterward, in Pamela's room, Elizabeth checked for ticks, looking carefully at her daughter's scalp, where they were most likely to hide.

"Mother, Grandfather didn't give me my rock back."

"Hmmm?" Elizabeth sounded abstracted.

"He didn't give me my rock back. I wanted to keep it."

"What do you want with a dirty rock, Pamela?"

"It was interesting. I found it. Ouch."

"Sorry, darling. Hold your head still, then I won't pull your hair."

"What did he mean when he said 'evidence'? Why would he want to bring archaeologists here?"

"He wants to dig up the hills."

"Dig them up? Oh. You mean to see if other things like the rock are buried there."

"That's right."

"And to find out about the people who built the hills."

"Yes. But he's been trying to get someone interested in this place for years and years. I don't see why that rock would change anything. And even if someone was interested, I don't really think people want to spend money on that kind of thing now."

"I didn't know Grandfather was interested in archaeology."

"It's his great passion. He's been to Greece and Africa to work on digs. He did some work on some of the other hill sites in Arkansas."

"Other hill sites? You mean there are other hills like these?"

"Oh, yes. All over the South." Elizabeth gave Pamela's hair a final tug. "You can get dressed now, darling." She moved away, and sat down on Pamela's bed. After a moment, she said, "Pamela."

Pamela turned from the wardrobe. Elizabeth's face was serious, and she conveyed an air of determination. Pamela had felt since she came upstairs that Elizabeth wanted to say something; she had seemed to approach it several times and then move away again. "Yes, Mother?"

"Pamela, there's something I want to tell you, and I want you to pay attention."

Pamela nodded.

"I don't want you going out into the woods alone again. Or to those hills."

Pamela thought of the strange panic that had gripped her after she found the rock, and the rustling she had heard in the underbrush. Thinking about it in the bath, she had decided both were only her imagination. Under Elizabeth's steady regard, she was suddenly not so sure. "Why not?"

"Use your head, darling. I just took three ticks off you. Besides ticks, there are mosquitoes and blackflies, black widow spiders under logs, and rattlesnakes in the underbrush. There's poison ivy and poison oak and poison sumac. There are gullies you can fall into and break your leg, not to mention crazy moonshiners with stills out in the clearings and sawed-off shotguns. There's even packs of wild dogs. When I was a child, they used to come into the yard at night and try to get at the chickens. They'll attack anything that moves."

Wild dogs, Pamela thought. Maybe she really had heard rustling in the bushes. Maybe she had been just a few feet from a pack of wild dogs. . . . She shuddered.

"I'll never go out there alone again, Mother, I promise."

"Good." Elizabeth got to her feet. "Now. Finish dressing, and then go into my room and put some cream on your face. You're very sunburnt. I don't want you to get too brown."

She left the room, closing the door softly behind her. Pamela finished tying her shoes and then sought out Elizabeth's dressing table, selecting the proper cream from the array of cosmetics that covered it. In the mirror her face looked unfamiliar, puffy and red. There were scratches on her cheeks.

Descending the stairs for supper, Pamela felt the nightly routine close numbingly around her. More than ever the house seemed like a dark cage. The hills rose in her mind from their cradle of silver grass, drenched in honey-colored sun, replete with mystery and possibility. She realized how very much she wanted to visit them again. But between the hills and the house lay the woods, with all its terrors. And so she would obey her mother. She would not return.

Chapter SIX

Summer arrived in early May. The days were hot and humid and drenched with sun. Rambler roses bloomed, passed their prime, and scattered multicolored petals over the ground. Spring bulbs withered, and the brilliant flowers of summer took their place: nasturtiums, marigolds, sweet william, hollyhocks, snapdragons, lilies, hydrangeas. The back garden overflowed with them, and every few days Sam brought armfuls up to the house for Elizabeth to arrange in vases and set around the rooms.

The pace of life changed with the heat, drawing in, becoming dark and slow. Shutters were pulled at noon, submerging the rooms in sepia-colored dimness; sun lanced through the slats, stratifying the heavy air with bars of gold. The hottest part of the day, between noon and three o'clock, was spent indoors, often in sleep. Supper was eaten later now, in the relative cool of twilight. Evening hours were passed on the porch, to take advantage of the slight breezes that sprang up with the darkness.

Accustomed to the leisurely New England seasons, Pamela could not get used to this abrupt and fierce change. She had never experienced heat like this, day after day after day without relief. No northern sky had ever been so metallic—she grew to hate the hazy light that bleached color out of things and laid a milky obscurity over the distance. No northern night had ever been so loud, filled with the unceasing cadence of crickets and katydids. During the day the insect-song was obscured by other noises, but at night it overwhelmed the ear, an undulating sheet of sound blanketing the entire world.

In school, despite open windows and ceiling fans, the heat was stupefying. Students, barely listening to the interminable lessons, slumped at desks whose varnish became unpleasantly tacky as the temperature rose. Pamela passed the long hours in a kind of daze. Her isolation was unassailable, like something carved in stone.

She had looked forward to summer vacation; but when school finally let out in June, Pamela found that freedom was even worse than bondage. Without school and homework her life became one long lonely weekend.

Often she watched wistfully as groups of girls passed by on the street outside. She imagined their activities: They might be going to Woolworth's, to have an ice-cream soda at the counter, or to a double-feature matinee at the movie theater, or to the swimming hole that lay at the outskirts of the town, or maybe just to each others' houses, to sit in the yards or on the porches with glasses of iced tea. It seemed impossible that a year ago, Pamela had been part of such pleasant pursuits. It felt like a lifetime.

Occasionally Pamela looked toward the trees massed at the bottom of the garden. She remembered the freedom of her afternoon among them, the light and the air and the swift passage of time. She felt the urge to venture down the path again, to escape the house and her boredom and loneliness. But she also remembered the rustling in the underbrush, the wild dogs and rattlesnakes. And so, although she sometimes stood on the veranda and gazed in what she imagined was the direction of the hills, she never set her feet upon the path she had followed that single time.

One night in mid-June, Pamela's grandfather made an announcement.

"I've some good news, Elizabeth."

Elizabeth looked up from her dessert. "What's that, Father?"

"You remember John Brinckerhoff, don't you?"

"John Brinckerhoff? Oh yes, the professor. The one you were in Greece with."

"That's right. He's chairman of the anthropology department at Indiana University now. I've been in touch with him about that fragment Pamela found—" He glanced at Pamela, and smiled very slightly. "It seems it was just the thing. He'll be sending a full team. They'll be here in two weeks."

"What?" Elizabeth's coffee cup had stopped halfway to her lips. She was staring at her father.

"He's going to establish a dig at the hills. You recall, I'm sure, that Brinckerhoff always shared my opinion about them."

"But you've been trying to do this for years. No one's ever been interested before."

"I never had evidence before. The people Brinckerhoff showed the fragment to were very impressed. They agree that the carving is typical of the Mound Cultures and provides very strong indication of habitation. And the extraordinary state of preservation would seem to indicate that these hills have not been disturbed or robbed. That's extremely rare, as you know. There might even be the possibility of finding an intact tomb. Think of it, Elizabeth. Think what a significant discovery that would be."

Pamela had never seen him so animated. Elizabeth was frowning. She lowered her coffee cup with a sharp *clink* of china.

"But you have no proof the fragment came from the hills. Pamela found it lying on the grass. There was no digging, no disturbance. It could have come from anywhere."

"How would it have gotten there, Elizabeth? Do you think birds carried it? Though I must admit I thought of that argument. I told Brinckerhoff I'd been digging myself."

"Oh, Father, I can't believe it." Elizabeth shook her head. Unaccountably, she sounded as if she were becoming angry. "Why do you spend your time this way?"

"You know how much I've always wanted to dig those hills, Elizabeth."

"There's a depression on. People are starving in the streets. How can anyone spend money on something like this? Think how many soup kitchens you could supply with the money this dig will take. Think how many people you could feed."

"The dig will be financed through the Works Progress Administration." Pamela's grandfather's voice was frosty. "It will provide work for jobless people. Not to mention the jobs and business it will create here in Flat Hills."

"It's a waste of money and a waste of time. You know very well you should leave those hills alone."

"Elizabeth." There was a strange inflection in his voice—

not anger, not anything Pamela could identify.

"Don't 'Elizabeth' me," Elizabeth snapped. A flush had spread across her cheekbones. "Did it occur to you how much trouble this will cause among the Indians? Those hills belong—they think those hills belong to them. How do you think they'll react if you start digging them up?"

"Of all the things that might give me reason to hesitate, that is the very least."

"Think of my mother, then. Think how she would feel if she were alive."

"Don't bring your mother into this, Elizabeth." His voice was very cold. "You don't know what she would have wanted."

"Don't I?" Elizabeth leaned forward; the sudden fury in her tone shocked Pamela. "I'd know better than you! You abandoned her, remember? You went off to Africa and Greece, you dug in the dirt while she grieved herself to death. *I* was the one who watched that happen. *I* was the one she talked to at the end. So don't you tell me I don't know—"

"Elizabeth!" His voice was like a whip. "I will not hear any more!"

For a moment the scene was frozen. Elizabeth, half out of her seat, her beautiful face suddenly pale; Pamela's grandfather, rigid as the chair he sat in. Then, all at once, the tension went out of Elizabeth's body. She sank back into her chair and put a hand to her eyes.

"I'm sorry, Father," she said. Her voice was low and trembled slightly, but it was her normal tone, not the barely controlled cry of a few moments before. "That was unforgivable."

"Perhaps you should go to your room, Elizabeth." The anger had gone from him too, and his tone was quiet.

"Yes. Yes, perhaps I should." She got up and placed her napkin beside her plate. She did not look at Pamela as she left the room. Pamela heard the staccato of her heels on the stairs.

Pamela sat very still, her eyes on her plate.

"I'm sorry you had to hear that, Pamela."

Her grandfather was regarding her with his deep-set eyes. Pamela saw, with some surprise, that he meant what he said.

"Your grandmother and I . . . we had difficulties. Your mother blames me for much of what went wrong between us. Perhaps she's right. Perhaps." He smiled, the slightest movement of his lips, somehow conveying bitterness. "I imagine she's told you something of this already. But there's more than one side to every story, Pamela. Your mother's bitterness clouds her perception. Try not to judge me too harshly."

Pamela looked at him. It had never occurred to her that he might care what she thought of him.

"Mother never really told me anything at all, Grandfather," she said. "All the time I was growing up, she never talked about her childhood or her mother or . . . or you."

He was still watching her. "Do you know, I didn't even learn you had been born until you were five years old. You must have wondered why I never sent you letters or presents. But your mother made it clear that she did not want me to be part of your life. I didn't wish to interfere."

Pamela said nothing. For most of her life she had barely thought of her grandfather, let alone wondered about him. Elizabeth had excised him from her life; she had excised him from Pamela's too. But he was a person, a person with feelings. Pamela thought of those cards arriving, unfailingly, on Christmas and on her mother's birthday. She knew for certain now that Elizabeth's long silence had hurt him.

By mutual consent they abandoned their half-finished desserts. Pamela's grandfather went back to his office. Pamela made her way upstairs. On the landing she hesitated for a little while before her mother's door, uncertain whether to intrude. At last she knocked. There was a pause, and then she heard Elizabeth's soft "Come in."

Elizabeth had retired to bed. She lay against propped-up pillows, her hair falling loose, the creamy lace of her negligee framing her shoulders. She was reading. The bedside lamp cast a soft glow across the coverlet.

"Hello, darling." Elizabeth seemed composed, but her face and voice were weary.

"Hello, Mother." Pamela seated herself on the edge of the bed. She looked at the shadows under Elizabeth's eyes, at the frown-creases on her forehead, and found she did not know what to say. It was Elizabeth who broke the silence.

"Pamela, I want to apologize for tonight."

"Mother—"

Elizabeth held up a hand. "No, let me finish. I shouldn't have let myself get so angry. It wasn't fair to you. It won't happen again, I promise."

"It's all right, Mother," Pamela said. She had not come here for an apology. "Really, it's all right."

Elizabeth held out her arms. "Come here."

Pamela leaned forward into Elizabeth's silk-clad arms. She rested her head on the soft skin of her mother's shoulder; the subtle mixed scents of Shalimar and face creams and skin-lightening preparations enfolded her. After a moment Elizabeth pushed her away gently.

"All right now?" she asked.

Pamela nodded. "Mother . . ." She hesitated. "Mother, why *did* you get angry?"

Elizabeth looked down at the coverlet.

"Those hills were very special to my mother," she said at last. "Part of the Indian traditions she was raised with. They used to quarrel about that—when I was a child, my father was very active in trying to get someone interested in excavating, but my mother believed the hills should be left alone. When he said the archaeologists were coming, now, after all these years, all I could think of was my mother, and how she would have hated what he's doing." Elizabeth sighed. "That was what made me angry, Pamela. But anger doesn't do any good—not to my mother, nor me either. It makes no difference what they do to those hills. No difference at all."

She sounded as if she were telling herself something she did not quite believe. For a moment she was silent, her expression indrawn, as if she were thinking of the past. She looked utterly drained.

"Darling, I think I'll go to sleep now," she said. "I really am exhausted."

Pamela got to her feet. She leaned down to kiss Elizabeth's cheek. "I love you, Mother."

"I love you too," Elizabeth whispered. She reached out her hand and let it rest for a moment against Pamela's face.

Pamela undressed, brushed her teeth and washed her face,

and got into bed with a book. The window was open; the stifling air moved sluggishly through it, and the voice of the insects rose and fell outside.

But she could not concentrate on reading. Her mind chased itself in circles: She could not stop thinking about her mother, her grandfather, her grandmother, the pattern they formed. There was so much more to Elizabeth's past than Pamela could ever have imagined. How could Elizabeth have kept everything hidden so thoroughly for so many years, almost as if she had no past at all? More and more it seemed to Pamela that she did not know her mother nearly as well as she had always thought.

It was an unsettling idea. To escape it Pamela turned her mind to the coming excavation. It must be interesting to be an archaeologist—digging down into the dark ground in order to bring to light relics from the past, searching out the bones of history. Could it really be that something so exotic as a lost civilization had existed here, in boring, ordinary Flat Hills? Her grandfather had mentioned a tomb. What exactly did that mean? Skeletons? Mummies and treasure, like in Egypt?

Beyond her open window she could see the indigo sky, bright with pinprick stars. Out there in the night lay the hills. She thought of the time she had visited them, of the sense she had received of oldness, of secrets, of mystery. It came to Pamela, suddenly, that her mother and her grandmother and the Indians were wrong. She did not know how she knew this, but she did. The past should not be buried in darkness. The hills should be opened, opened to the light.

Chapter SEVEN

Over the next two weeks, preparations for the dig gathered momentum. Every night at supper Pamela's grandfather provided Pamela and Elizabeth with an update on the day's progress, displaying an animation and volubility of which Pamela would not have believed him capable.

"I've arranged for the archaeologists to stay at the hotel here in town," he told them. "They'll take their meals at local restaurants and buy their supplies in local stores. The team will include only the director and his assistants, which means that the unskilled diggers, the haulers, the cooks, and everyone else at the site can be hired right here in Flat Hills. And there'll be plenty of other work—the team will need laundry done, their vehicles will need fuel, and I've already hired a crew to widen the road out to the hills. You see, Elizabeth, far from being a drain on our country's resources, the dig will bring work and business to this town. People here are very happy about that, I can tell you."

Elizabeth, who had been calmly eating dessert during this recital, smiled slightly.

"I don't doubt it, Father. Especially as so much of the cost seems to be coming out of your own pocket."

Her grandfather seemed to take Elizabeth's gentle mockery in stride. Discussion of the dig no longer elicited any other reaction from her. If anything, she seemed bored.

"I listened to so much archaeology talk when I was growing up," she explained to Pamela. "My mind just goes numb when I hear it now. I can't imagine anything more unpleasant than grubbing in the dirt under the broiling sun for little pieces of stone and pottery. But for your grandfather it's the most fascinating thing in the world. He can't imagine that anyone could feel any different. You must pretend to be interested, darling, just to be polite."

But Pamela did not have to pretend. She really was interested. She found it fascinating to think that an entire civilization had sprung up and passed away centuries before her own birth. The people who had lived on the hills were gone, but the hills still stood, a shadow cast by the past upon the present. Once the excavation started, once the hills were opened, once the artifacts were brought into the light and the process of learning began, it would be as if those lost people had regained their voices, and could speak again, clearly, in present time. Pamela wanted very much to hear what they would say.

Pamela's grandfather was pleased by her interest and took to addressing much of his suppertime conversation to her. An amateur archaeologist all his life, he had made a particular study of the Mound Culture, participating in a number of other excavations, even publishing articles in learned journals. He answered all Pamela's questions, which she asked timidly at first, but with more confidence as it became clear that he really did not mind explaining things. At these times he seemed quite different from the taciturn, aloof man who usually sat at the supper table, and Pamela often found herself forgetting how awkward he had once made her feel.

"The Mound Culture was extensive," he told Pamela, "and flourished for several hundred years. Its people had a well-developed religion, and their artistic skills were excellent. They built dozens of hill-sites, all across the South. Mostly these are flat-topped pyramids, like the ones here, but in some cases there are also great circular earthworks. There are even sites where animal forms have been built out of earth."

"How were they built, Grandfather?" Pamela asked.

"We think they carried the earth in baskets, dumped it out on the site, and packed it down with their feet or with stones or pieces of wood."

"They carried all that dirt by hand?" Pamela was awed. She tried to imagine how many baskets of soil it would take to build the hills. Thousands, surely. Maybe millions.

"Not only that, but they were able to achieve very precise measurements. Many of the hills are symmetrical to within a few inches. And the hills here are small in comparison with others—in Illinois, for instance, or Alabama. It's quite an astonishing achievement."

"What were the hills for? Did they live on them?"

"No. The people lived in villages nearby. The hills were for worship. We don't know much about their religion, except that it involved a recurring set of symbols, which are seen in artifacts from nearly all the hill-sites. It's possible they practiced human sacrifice, like the Aztecs or the Incas. Their art certainly has something in common with those cultures."

"Human sacrifice," repeated Pamela, fascinated. "Why would they sacrifice people?"

"The Aztecs sacrificed to honor their sun god. They believed he needed human blood to drink."

"Really, Father," said Elizabeth fastidiously.

"Remember, Pamela, you can't judge ancient civilizations by the standards you and I would use today. They were pagans, after all. They knew no better. They didn't have the Christian values that are necessary if a culture is to survive."

Pamela thought of the empty hills, the abandoned valley. "And the Mound People didn't survive."

"No. They disappeared about five centuries ago."

"Just . . . disappeared?"

"Yes. It might have been warfare, or maybe some kind of plague. We don't really know. You have to understand, Pamela, that nearly everything about the Mound People is mysterious at this point. We have very little concrete information. Many of the smaller hill-sites have been destroyed by building over, or by farmers plowing them up for fields. Many of the larger ones were vandalized, or robbed, or badly excavated by amateurs. That's why this excavation is so important. My hope is that it will provide a model for others, and I am certain that it will substantially expand our knowledge of the Mound Culture. In fact, I firmly believe that this will be one of the most significant excavations ever carried out in the United States."

"Oh, Father," Elizabeth said. "Don't you think you're exaggerating a little?"

"Absolutely not, Elizabeth." His voice was completely serious. "Mark my words. We will find artifacts at this site to eclipse all other Mound Culture discoveries."

These conversations filled Pamela's head with fantastic images—she imagined dark underground passages, mysterious stone rooms, complex carvings, jewelry of silver and copper and turquoise and pearl. At such times she could hardly wait for the dig to begin. She had even begun to dream about it: Now and then, waking abruptly, she would be left with vague, floating images of torches, scintillating mica, flashing copper, the beaks of birds.

On a sweltering afternoon in late June, the archaeologists arrived. Pamela's grandfather had been off since early morning seeing to final arrangements, and when he returned he brought with him the director of the team, Dr. Carl Weber. Dr. Weber was a small, thin man somewhere in middle age, with blond hair and skin tanned a dark leathery brown. He had small, rather prominent eyes of a peculiarly brilliant blue green. His hands were large and calloused and darker even than his face, as if permanently stained with the earth of his profession. He spoke with the trace of a foreign accent and was enormously polite.

"I have invited Dr. Weber to stay with us, Elizabeth," Pamela's grandfather said after introductions had been made. "It will be much more comfortable than the hotel. I've ordered his things to be brought up."

Elizabeth smiled graciously. "You are welcome in our home, Dr. Weber. I'll see that a room is made up for you."

They sat down to supper. Dr. Weber and Pamela's grandfather conversed about the dig. At least a week would be taken up with preliminary work: making a map of the site, taking measurements, setting up equipment and tents, and doing things called "gridding" and "core sampling." Much of the talk was too technical for Pamela to fully understand, but the very mystery lent fascination.

As Esther cleared away the plates and prepared to serve dessert, Dr. Weber turned politely to Elizabeth.

"Please accept my apologies for monopolizing the conversation, Mrs. Martin," he said. "It must be very dull for you."

"No apology is needed." Elizabeth smiled with all her charm. She looked very beautiful tonight, animated by the presence of a guest, even one who talked about archaeology. "You and my father have many important things to discuss, I know."

Dr. Weber inclined his head. "You are very kind." He looked toward Pamela. "Your daughter certainly seems interested in it all."

Pamela felt herself blush.

"I've been telling her about the preparations," said Pamela's grandfather.

"It must seem very strange to you, my dear, a lot of grown men digging in the dirt."

"Oh, no," Pamela said. "I think it must be awfully interesting to be an archaeologist."

"Do you indeed!" Dr. Weber smiled at her, without condescension. "Perhaps you'd like to pay a visit to the site. That is, if it is all right with you, Mrs. Martin. Her grandfather could bring her along one day this week. She'd be quite safe, I assure you."

"Oh, Mother, could I?" Pamela could not restrain her eagerness.

Elizabeth's brows creased slightly, and for just an instant

Pamela was afraid she would refuse. But then she nodded.

"I'll hold you to that, Dr. Weber," she said. "Yes, Pamela, you can go."

For the rest of the meal, the conversation was of more general matters. Pamela heard none of it; she was in a haze of excitement. In a few days she would see what she had been imagining for weeks. In a few days she would be at the hills once more.

That night Pamela dreamed, a strange, uneasy dream. She thought she was on the hill again, and someone with eyes like Elizabeth's was watching her from a little distance away. She searched the short grass for the fragment of rock, but nowhere could she see the flash of mica. Where was the fragment now? she wondered in her dream. What had her grandfather done with it?

Chapter EIGHT

Pamela sat beside her grandfather in his large black car. The windows were open; a hot breeze lifted the hair from her cheeks. The car drew a comet-tail of dust behind it. Since the middle of June it had been very dry, and the trees and bushes on each side of the road were filmed with dust. The air quivered with heat. Sweat ran down Pamela's sides beneath her cotton dress, and her throat was already dry. But discomfort was not enough to quell her excitement, which had been rising since this morning. In just a few minutes, she would see the dig.

The evening before, her mother had extracted a promise from Pamela.

"I want you to stay close to your grandfather," she had said, her face serious. "You remember what I told you about how dangerous it can be out there, don't you? Well, it's safe if you're with someone, but you mustn't go off on your own. You must stay with your grandfather, every minute. Will you promise to do that?"

Pamela nodded. "I promise."

"And don't speak to any strangers. Heaven knows who he's hired to work out there—probably all the riffraff in town."

"Mother . . . thank you for letting me go out to the site. I . . . I hope you don't mind."

Elizabeth raised her perfectly penciled eyebrows. "Why should I mind? You'll be quite safe with your grandfather."

"It's not that. I was just thinking about what you said about your mother. How the hills were special to her."

"Pamela." Elizabeth took Pamela's hand. "You're very sweet. But you mustn't think I'm still upset about that. I was tired that night, I wasn't myself. It was very silly of me to react that way."

And she was gone. But she left behind the image of her worried eyes. Since the night of the quarrel, Elizabeth had reacted to the dig with nothing stronger than boredom. But Pamela knew her mother. Pamela was certain that, no matter what she said, Elizabeth did mind her visit to the excavation site.

The dirt road leading to the valley turned off the main road at a sharp angle. It was plain it had been newly cut—its edges were rough and raw, and white stumps showed where the trees and underbrush had been hacked back. Pamela's grandfather slowed the car, trying to avoid the deep ruts.

Abruptly they emerged on the crest of the valley. Pamela, who had expected the same empty vista, received a shock. The valley was barely recognizable as the peaceful place she had stumbled on many weeks ago. Men had overrun the hills. There were vehicles of every description, mules and horses, piles of equipment and supplies. A long wooden shed with a tarpaulin roof was being completed, its boards as raw as the newly turned soil beside the road. There were several smaller sheds, and a few pitched tents. A big trestle table had been set up beneath a second tarpaulin.

All of this Pamela absorbed in the instant it took to crest the edge of the valley and begin the descent. The road became a set of wheel marks in the flattened grass, and the car bumped slowly over the uneven ground. They drew to a stop beside the long shed. Pamela's grandfather turned off the engine, and its purr was replaced by the many sounds of men at work. In the odd stillness of this place, they seemed abnormally loud. It was breathlessly hot.

Pamela's grandfather got out of the car. In place of his usual formal, perfectly pressed business clothes, he wore old khaki trousers that were baggy in the knees and seat, frayed suspenders, a faded collarless shirt, and a soft-brimmed hat. He surveyed the site, his stance easy and relaxed.

Following her grandfather out of the car, Pamela saw that Dr. Weber was already hurrying toward them, wiping his forehead with a bandanna. He held out his hand.

"Welcome, welcome," he said. "I am so glad you could both be here on our first day of work. Of course, it's all preliminaries at this point, nothing really exciting. . . . Shall I give you a tour?"

"I believe my granddaughter would enjoy that. What do you say, Pamela?"

"Yes, thank you. I'd love it."

"Very well. Follow me."

Dr. Weber took off, trailing a stream of words. He explained everything in the greatest detail; Pamela felt she was absorbing only a fraction of it all. Nevertheless she learned that many of the men were engaged in creating a topographical map of the area; that the piles of equipment contained not only specialized digging tools but tools that would allow preliminary restoration and preservation; and that, besides the diggers, there were a number of people whose sole task would be to number, catalog, and write detailed descriptions of every single artifact found, no matter how small.

This was what would go on inside the long shed, where tables were set up ready to receive whatever the site yielded. The tents were for sleeping: At least three men would be here at all times to guard the site and its contents. The smaller sheds, sturdily built with padlocking doors, would be used for storage of the more valuable items.

The tour took them over the whole site, from sheds to tarpaulins to equipment. Pamela's grandfather kept pace with Dr. Weber, showing the greatest interest and asking many questions; Pamela tried to keep up but was frequently left behind. The sun burned the top of her head, despite her sun hat. Dust was everywhere, acrid in the nose and throat, irritating to the eyes, coating the busy sunburnt workers.

Dr. Weber mopped his face frequently with his bandanna; his blue work shirt was soaked through. Only Pamela's grandfather seemed unaffected, moving easily through the debris and confusion, completely at home. Pamela noticed that he seemed to know most of the workers: Beneath Dr. Weber's explanations her grandfather carried on a constant subtext of greeting and comment. The men replied respectfully, removing their hats and bobbing their heads.

At last they reached the central hill. Dr. Weber explained how it would be mapped and gridded and dug in small sections. Digging must never be random, he explained. Precise sites must be prepared, and the earth must be removed fraction by fraction, with the utmost delicacy, so that nothing would be missed or damaged. The very pebbles, even holes in the ground, could be of enormous significance. Dr. Weber demonstrated the special tools that would be used—small wedge-shaped trowels, spatulate knives, soft brushes, even spoons. All the earth taken from the site would be carefully kept and sieved, so that it could be reexamined for any tiny secrets that might have been overlooked.

At this point, the talk became technical, liberally laced with words and phrases like "middens," "flint-kernel corn," "celts," "Clovis points," and "postholes." Pamela felt that she had been forgotten. She looked out over the dig. In spite of herself she was beginning to feel bored. It was very different from the way she had imagined it—so hot, so dirty, so . . . ugly. Men scurried everywhere, clouds of ocher dust rose from the constantly moving vehicles, debris littered the once-pristine grass. This valley did not feel like the place she had discovered that warm day in April. She could still see that place in her mind, empty and silent, opening out as if for her alone. She was standing in almost the same spot where she had fallen asleep, yet she could find no trace of the mystery she had sensed.

Pamela felt perspiration trickling down her cheeks and neck; she was so hot she could hardly stand it, and her mouth felt like a dustbowl. At last Dr. Weber seemed to become aware of her discomfort.

"Why don't you go get yourself a drink of water, my dear? There's a barrel under the tarp over there."

Pamela made her way down the hill, past groups of men, dodging the occasional car or horse-drawn cart. In the shade of the tarpaulin she drank several dippers of water. She moistened her handkerchief and used it to wipe some of the dust from her face. It occurred to her that she was already breaking her promise to remain by her grandfather's side. Never mind, she thought, she could still see him atop the hill, talking with Dr. Weber.

A boy was working near the tarpaulin, unloading boxes from the back of a truck and stacking them inside one of the locking sheds. He looked toward her each time he passed. He wore faded overalls and a tattered straw hat; he was an Indian. There was something annoyingly bold in his regard, as if he knew her from somewhere and thought she should know him.

After a few moments Pamela left the shade of the tarpaulin, seeking escape from the valley as much as from the boy's watchful eyes. She trudged across the tangled grass toward the trees at the valley's rim. She sat down just within the shade of the first fringe of forest, removing her sun hat and letting the breeze ruffle her hair. It was amazing how much hotter it was down in the valley; some odd inversion of the air seemed to magnify the sun like a burning glass. Dreamily she gazed at the activity below. The sounds were oddly muffled. The whole scene looked unreal. She could see the damage summer had worked on this place: The silvery grass had dried to a pale brittle gold, and all the wildflowers were gone.

There were an unusual number of crows around the site; she had noticed them in the valley, pecking boldly here and there, flying out of the way only if someone got too close.

There were even more of them up here, dotted about the periphery as if they too were watching the proceedings below. They were the biggest birds Pamela had ever seen, with sharp yellow beaks and sooty black feathers that turned iridescent in the sun. They stalked backward and forward on restless feet, cawing occasionally, as if commenting to one another.

Abruptly Pamela was seized by uneasiness, as compelling as it was irrational. There was something about the massed birds she did not like—perhaps it was the sheer number of them as much as their size and their strangely sentient croaking. Carefully she got to her feet and began to descend into the valley, feeling, absurdly, that there were eyes upon her back. The blistering heat enclosed her, noise and dust enveloped her. The breeze—and the birds—were left behind.

Pamela could no longer see her grandfather or Dr. Weber, so she returned to the tarpaulin and sat down to wait. The watching boy was gone; no one else took any notice of her.

At last her grandfather appeared, deep in conversation with Dr. Weber.

"There you are, Pamela," he said when he saw her. "I'm sorry to keep you waiting here. Was it very long?"

"No, Grandfather." But it had been; it had felt like forever.

Her grandfather drank a dipperful of water, and then extended his hand to Dr. Weber.

"Weber, thank you for your time this afternoon. It's been most rewarding. We'll be seeing a lot of each other in the next few weeks."

"Indeed." Polite as he was, Dr. Weber was unmistakably

anxious to be elsewhere. "I appreciate your interest and assistance. Now, I've a great deal to do—I can leave you to make your own way out?"

And he hurried purposefully off. Pamela's grandfather led the way back to the car. Inside, it was so hot that for a moment Pamela's breath was taken away. She could feel the black leather of the seats burning her legs through the thin cotton of her dress. Her grandfather pressed the starter, turned the car in a wide arc, and began to guide it up the track.

A little group of people stood at the crest of the valley, at the edge of the newly cut road. There were six of them. Pamela could see, as the car approached, that they were all Indians. The four men wore patched shirts and shabby overalls; they were indistinguishable from the local country-folk except for their coppery skin and raven black hair, which most wore much longer than was customary. One man had braids that came halfway down his chest. One of the women was young, her long black tresses loose down her back. The other was old. Her gray braids were bound with leather, and she wore an ankle-length skirt with multicolored flounces. Pamela craned forward for a better view as the car passed, and the old woman turned. Pamela received a swift impression of a lined face and sharp dark eyes.

The car reached the main road and began to move faster. Cooler air blew through the window, dispelling some of the stifling heat.

"You saw that group of Indians back there."

Pamela started a little. "Yes, Grandfather."

"Do you know, I offered them jobs—I was willing to pay

good wages too. But they all refused, except for one young man." He shook his head. "Such is the power of their superstition."

"You mean about the hills?" Pamela asked.

He glanced at her. "Has your mother told you about the hills?"

There was something in his tone Pamela could not interpret. "She said they were important to the Indians, but she didn't really explain why."

Her grandfather nodded. His eyes remained on the road. "The Indians have a legend that their ancestors built the hills," he said. "It's very complicated, with blood sacrifices and totems and evil priests and dream-journeys, but basically the Indians believe an ancestor of theirs is buried in the valley, and the grave mustn't be disturbed. It's pretty farfetched in this day and age, of course, but to them it's gospel truth. Still, these legends do sometimes have a kernel of fact behind them. I've always thought it offered some direction for archaeological study."

"Was it my grandmother who told you the legend?"

He looked toward her again. "Yes."

"Did she believe in the legend? Was that why she wouldn't have wanted the hills dug?"

For a moment he did not reply, being occupied with maneuvering the car around a large pothole. Outside the window, the dusty trees flowed past; ahead, the road dissolved into oily heat mirages. The pothole fell away behind them, but still the silence stretched on. Pamela glanced at him out of the corner of her eye. Had she said too much? Was he angry? She could read nothing from his face.

"You must understand," he said at last, "that my wife was an intelligent woman who wanted very much to escape the world she was born into. But somehow she was never able to fully do so. To this day I don't really understand why. For my sake she pretended, and for a long time I was fooled. What finally opened my eyes was her opposition to my efforts to get someone interested in excavating the hills. I assumed at first that it arose out of concern for the traditions and feelings of her people. But there was a darker reason. In her heart, she still believed in the legends. I know this because I asked her, and she told me so."

His hands were tight on the steering wheel, and his eyes gazed unblinking into the glare of the sun.

"It was . . . difficult. I tried so hard to help her change, you see. But she could not shut those hills out of her life. The hills, and the traditions that went with them. There is a terrible power to superstition, Pamela. I have seen the destruction it works. It blighted my wife's life. It destroyed our marriage. It even reached out for our daughter."

Pamela looked at him in surprise. "My mother?"

"Yes. My wife promised never to speak to Elizabeth of her Indian ways, and she kept her promise. But Elizabeth saw the trouble between us, heard the quarrels. It was hard for her. It made her angry, rebellious. When she was about thirteen I discovered that she had been visiting my wife's sister, who was feeding her all sorts of Indian nonsense. I put a stop to it of course, but Elizabeth was at an impressionable age, and the woman managed to exert quite an influence on her."

"She never told me about that."

"It was a bad time in all our lives, Pamela. My wife was

very ill—she died not long afterward. Perhaps Elizabeth wants to forget. God knows I wanted to, for a long time."

Pamela thought of the pain she had seen in Elizabeth's face when she spoke of her mother. That pain was mirrored now in her grandfather's voice.

"Elizabeth would like to keep the hills whole, in her mother's memory," Pamela's grandfather said. His words were soft—Pamela could barely hear them above the hum of the engine. "But I will open them in her memory. I will turn them inside out, strip them of all their secrets. When I am finished, there will be no legends left."

They drove the rest of the way in silence.

Pamela took a bath, washing away the dust and sweat of her afternoon among the hills, and went to her room to dress for dinner. She stood for a moment by her window, where the air was a little cooler. The sun was beginning to sink, and a wash of gold spread upward from the horizon. Birds were dark specks against the sky, wheeling above the trees, heading homeward for the night.

Pamela thought again of the strutting crows, their black feathers brushed with oily iridescence in the sun. She thought of the busy, dirty valley, the hills rising at its center. To the hills, old as they were, all this activity must seem no more than the smallest ripple in the unruffled stream of centuries. Belatedly some of the mystery she had felt when she first glimpsed them returned to her. And with it her grandfather's words, echoing strangely inside her head: *When I am finished, there will be no legends left.*

Chapter NINE

On the second day of the dig, Dr. Weber and his team began to sink shafts into the hills. These were deep holes, about a foot square, which would allow analysis of the internal configurations of the ground. The shafts revealed an unusual fact. Dr. Weber spoke about it over supper toward the end of the week, using technical terms that Pamela could only dimly grasp. After a while, in his kind way, he turned to make an explanation for her benefit.

"Strata, my dear, are the different layers of the earth seen in cross section. In this context, they refer to the levels where the remains of the Mound People appear. Most often, the hill-sites were used for decades, sometimes for centuries. Periodically the temples or buildings that stood on them would be destroyed and a layer of earth built up above the remains. Another building would then be constructed on the new level. In most hill-sites there are as many as five strata. But in this site there is only one. Naturally, this will limit the number of remains we can find." He glanced at Pamela's grandfather. "I'm afraid this dig may not add much to the sum of our knowledge of the Mound People. It's a shame, after our high hopes for it."

"I think your assessment is a bit hasty, Weber," Pamela's grandfather said. "After all, the fact that there is only one occupancy makes the site unusual. I'm convinced it points to the extreme antiquity of the hills. It is assumed that the Mound Culture migrated to this area originally from the western part of the country. Could that not mean this place might be the point from which the culture spread, perhaps the very locus of the civilization?"

Dr. Weber shook his head. "Unlikely, in my view."

"Well." Pamela's grandfather smiled, with perfect good humor. "We shall see whom the coming days prove correct."

By Saturday of the first week, the shaft study was complete, and the site had been fully mapped. Sunday was a day of rest, even for Pamela's grandfather, though he seemed to chafe at the enforced inactivity.

On Monday the springy turf of the central hilltop was peeled back, and the bare earth divided into three sections. Each was further subdivided into small square subsections. The subsections were cleared to different levels—the once-flat hilltop now resembled a series of uneven stair steps—and a pair of diggers was assigned to each subsection, where they scraped at the ground with the small implements Dr. Weber had shown Pamela on her first visit.

Pamela's grandfather had been at the site daily since the beginning, but it was not until Tuesday of the second week that he brought Pamela with him again. He and Dr. Weber mounted the central hill, Pamela in tow; they were soon engrossed in a technical discussion.

Patiently Pamela followed them about. The heat was dreadful, worse than last time. Already the back of her dress and her hatband were soaked. Dust seemed to have gotten into her mouth—she could taste it on her tongue. How could the diggers stand it for eight hours a day, their backs bent beneath the merciless sun, moving earth aside a teaspoonful at a time? Their progress seemed agonizingly slow—at this rate it would take weeks, months even, to dig down any distance at all. Pamela found it increasingly difficult to maintain interest and ignore her discomfort. In spite of herself, her mind wandered. She thought of glasses of iced tea, the shade of a veranda, the feel of cool water against her skin.

Below, in the valley, there was a sudden eruption of agitated shouting. Pamela turned her head, shading her eyes against the glare. A knot of men was gathering near one of the large piles of dirt removed during the initial preparations for excavation. They formed a tight circle around something in their midst.

Dr. Weber rapidly descended the hill. Reaching the group, he pushed his way between the gathered men, Pamela and her grandfather behind him. One of the trucks used for hauling supplies was slewed round at an angle against the dirt pile. Against its side a man was propped, his head thrown back, his eyes closed. Pamela had just time to see his leg, bent at a strange angle, and his torn trousers, soaked with blood, before her grandfather seized her shoulders and turned her to face the opposite direction.

"Go sit in the water tent, Pamela," he said gently. "I'll come fetch you in a little while."

Pamela obeyed, feeling faint and a little sick. Brief as it was, the image of the injured man had imprinted itself on her brain like a photograph: his ashen face, his unnaturally bent leg, the red of his blood seeping into the ocher dirt beside him. And nearby, a dark shape—a crow. Pamela looked back.

Crows were perched all over the pile of earth that towered above the crowd, croaking and bobbing their heads, for all the world as if they were commenting on the turmoil below.

In the shade of the tent, Pamela drank some water and wiped her face. She sat down on a bench to wait. She fancied she could hear the rasping of the crows, somewhere beneath the noise of men and vehicles.

Pamela's grandfather came to fetch her at last. Leaving the site they passed the group of Indians—Pamela's grandfather told her they stood here every day. The old woman in the colorful skirt was among them. Pamela had the impression that the woman's eyes followed her as they moved slowly past, the car wheels jolting in the ruts of the dirt road. Beside her, her grandfather turned his head briefly in the woman's direction, and then away.

"Grandfather, is that man going to be all right?"

"His leg is broken, and he's lost some blood, but he'll recover. Dr. Weber has taken him to the hospital."

"How did it happen?"

"Apparently he was suffering from heatstroke. He fainted and fell in front of the truck. He's lucky he wasn't killed."

Pamela shuddered.

Dr. Weber and Pamela's grandfather discussed the incident at supper. Dr. Weber was obviously distressed.

"It's this heat," he said, shaking his head. "It makes the men careless and stupid. Till now it's been nothing more than sprained ankles and dropped equipment. But what happened today is serious. I feel that if we don't slow our pace there will be more accidents, maybe worse ones."

Pamela's grandfather frowned. "Slow our pace?"

"I've been thinking about it for several days. We must decrease the hours of work and give the men time off during the middle of the day, when the sun is hottest. And the scope of the operation must be scaled back, at least for now. I think it would be sensible to work just on the central hill and leave the smaller ones for later."

"But, Weber, we cannot allow the project to suffer! I agree with you about letting the men take a break, and so on. But to stop working on the smaller hills—"

Dr. Weber was shaking his head. His face was determined. "While this heat wave lasts, we stand to lose far more time to injuries and accidents than to judicious cuts in hours. The men are not happy about the working conditions anyway—a number have already complained to me. If we don't do something, not only will there be accidents, the men will become demoralized and resentful. If the heat breaks, I'll consider a return to a full schedule."

The two men looked at each other. Dr. Weber's blue green eyes were bright and narrow. It was a test of wills. Pamela felt the tension; Elizabeth, her hands nervously pleating her napkin, seemed aware of it also. After a very long moment, Pamela's grandfather capitulated.

"Very well, Weber," he said. "Until the heat breaks."

And so the weather assumed an unwelcome partnership in the process of excavation. Arkansas summers were always hot, but this summer was unusual. The minor dryness of June was, in July, becoming full-fledged drought. The once-green grass was bleached to parchment color; flowers and vegetables drooped, wheat and corn dried in the fields. Dust laid itself over every surface. At night, heat lightning rippled along the horizon, and illusory, stormless thunder punctuated the dark. But no rain fell, and the temperature continued to soar—95, 98, even 100 degrees.

In spite of Dr. Weber's precautions, the string of heat-related mishaps and misfortunes continued. Almost every day a worker collapsed, overcome by the sun; there were always three or four men on the sick list with various sun-induced illnesses. The ubiquitous dust fouled equipment and choked the engines of the trucks. Mule- and horse-drawn carts were brought in as substitutes; the animals, however, proved nearly as susceptible to the temperature as the diggers. Two more serious accidents occurred: One man was struck in the chest by a stone that flew up from beneath the wheels of one of the mule carts, and a second was pinned beneath a tent pole when one of the guy ropes for the cataloging tent snapped.

"I have worked in India and Greece and Egypt," Dr. Weber said, shaking his head, creases of concern furrowing his forehead. "Never have I seen so many foul-ups on a single dig."

Only the crows appeared immune to the valley's discomforts. They were everywhere, strutting about the site as if they owned it, their black feathers pristine amid the dust, their hoarse croaking constantly audible beneath the noise of work. Amazingly bold, they waddled into the tents, flew up from beneath the wheels of the carts—several times nearly causing accidents—fouled the ground with their guano, and vandalized any food left untended. At twilight they rose into the air, wheeling against the dimming sky, settling for the night like flakes of soot drifting down onto the tents, the dirt piles, the carts, the hilltops, every elevated surface.

Pamela's grandfather too was in his element: He seemed completely unaffected by the difficult conditions. At most a slight sheen of perspiration marked his cheeks. He gave the most minute attention to every aspect of the operation, from the actual archaeological work to the mens' noon meal—his patience, and his energy, seemed inexhaustible. Often Dr. Weber and his assistants visibly flagged, yet the worse the conditions grew, the more dynamic the older man became.

Pamela accompanied him every day now. Each visit was much like the last—they might inspect the diggers on the central hill, or visit the tent where the catalogers worked, or pore over maps and charts—but always there was the blazing sun, the pall of dust, the sweat, the thirst. More and more, Pamela took to seeking the sanctuary of the water tent, waiting there till her grandfather came to collect her.

Driving home in the hot car, she listened as he talked eagerly about the accomplishments of the day. The air roared like a blast furnace through the open windows, drying the sweat on her face and making her skin feel stiff and papery. At night in her bath, dust made a thin film on the water. Exhausted as she was after trips to the dig, she still found it difficult to fall asleep. She lay wakeful in the dark, sometimes for hours, listening to the rise and fall of the insect-song outside her window, longing for a breeze to lighten the thick and muggy air.

For Pamela, the magic conjured up by the dig had all but dissolved. There were no mysterious rooms, fabulous caches of carvings, pottery, silver or gold or turquoise; these things were no more than products of her imagination, called up out of ignorance. Now that she knew the reality—heat and dust;

dirt and sweat; boring, backbreaking, agonizingly slow work that seemed to produce nothing at all—the thought of the dig provoked not excitement or a sense of mystery but a feeling of aversion. She longed for the courage to tell this to her grandfather. But she knew he would not understand. It was not just that he was unable to imagine anyone who did not feel as he did. She knew her interest had come to be important to him.

Yet beneath simple boredom and discomfort ran something deeper. The accident Pamela had seen made a strong impression on her. Every time she returned to the hills, that memory brushed the place with horror. Sometimes as her grandfather's car crested the edge of the valley and began to bump down the track, Pamela felt actual fear constrict her throat. That fear was echoed and distorted in the strange, jumbled dreams that filled her restless nights, dreams whose images faded as soon as she awoke, so that she could never remember properly what she had dreamed, only that it was frightening.

Chapter TEN

At last, toward the end of the third week, the diggers began to make discoveries. A number of postholes were found— these, Dr. Weber explained, were the places where the supports of buildings had been planted. When their locations were plotted on a chart, it would become possible to speculate on how the hill had looked when it had been inhabited. In addition, great quantities of pottery shards began to appear. They were nothing more than small, jagged chunks of mud-colored clay, many with traces of incised designs, as ordinary and uncommunicative as the dirt they came from.

There were other discoveries too, more mysterious and more interesting, and more valuable. They were kept in the locked sheds, but Dr. Weber sometimes brought a few home with him for further study. One evening after supper, he displayed some of these artifacts on the glossy surface of the dining table.

He laid out first a quantity of small, wafer-thin arrowheads and knife blades fashioned from flint and other, darker stones. They had distinctively long, leaflike shapes, and, even after centuries of interment, light glinted sharp along their edges, announcing their original deadly purpose. Next came several small clay figurines in the forms of animals and birds, hollow or bearing bowls on their heads and backs, like pipes or whistles. They were astonishingly well modeled. Even the blunting of time could not erase the delicate shaping of wing and paw. Finally, with infinite care, Dr. Weber laid out the prize of the collection: a necklace of copper and pearls, blackened and verdigrised by its long tenure in the earth, but beautiful nonetheless.

Pamela gazed upon these objects. This was more like what she had imagined before the dig had begun. What a weight of time the artifacts represented! The people of the valley had made these things, she thought. Centuries ago they had held them in their hands. What secrets did they guard? What lives had those arrowheads pierced, what long-dead woman had worn that necklace?

All at once the little objects on the table seemed dark, saturated with age. For just an instant, Pamela seemed to feel the weight of earth that had covered them, blinding, stifling, unbearably heavy. . . .

Dr. Weber and Pamela's grandfather were bent over the table, deep in discussion. Beside them Elizabeth stood absolutely still, holding a cup of coffee in her hand. She was staring fixedly at the artifacts. Pamela looked at her face. In it she seemed to see a mirror image of her own emotions.

Insight flashed into Pamela's mind. Elizabeth was not bored by the dig. She was afraid of it.

Elizabeth looked up. She met Pamela's eyes. There was a fractional pause, and then she smiled. The strange look was gone. Gracefully she turned and put her coffee cup on the sideboard. Without glancing at the table again, she moved from the room, seating herself in the parlor and taking up her needlepoint.

Pamela's sudden understanding had receded even as she perceived it. Now it seemed implausible, absurd. She put a hand to her forehead. She was tired, that was it. It had been a long, hot day. She needed to sleep.

She said good night to her grandfather and Dr. Weber—they barely noticed—and went upstairs to her room. She undressed and got into bed with a book, but she was too tired to read. She turned out the light and closed her eyes.

Pamela dreamed.

She was standing on a large, flat, elevated plain, at one end of an avenue of torches. It was the place she had dreamed of the afternoon she had fallen asleep on the hill. She could see the great square building that rose at the end of the plain. It had high walls, a flat, thatched roof, and massive pillars that supported each of the corners and framed the doorway. The pillars were elaborately carved or painted, but Pamela was too far away to make out the designs.

Pamela sensed, out in the night, the presence of many people. She could hear them shifting and whispering, yet try as she might she could not see them in the darkness. The soft hissing of their voices hovered just beyond the edge of understanding; either they spoke too softly or their language was not familiar.

There was a stirring within the dark spaces of the building, and a figure emerged into the torchlight. It was a man, tall, yet dwarfed by the massive scale of the doorway behind him. He descended the steps that led to the flat ground of the hilltop, walking unhurriedly. Pamela recognized him as the man of her first dream. He wore a feathered cloak and a high, feathered headdress, and around his hips was a kind of pleated kilt ending just above the knee. He wore a curved breastplate of bone or ivory, and laced sandals. On his arm was a great gold band. His face was hidden by the sharp-beaked mask of a bird.

Pamela stood still as the man approached her. Again she had the impression that he knew her, and this time she felt she knew him too, though she could not quite recall who he was. He was closer now, closer than he had been in her previous dream. He stopped. The mask regarded her impassively, the torchlight flickering along its painted planes. Within the eyeholes Pamela saw the flash of a living gaze. He began to lift his hand.

The completion of the gesture was lost: Pamela found herself, abruptly, awake. The stifling air was close around her; her sheets were uncomfortably twisted. She threw them off and lay staring at the ceiling.

It had not quite been a nightmare, but it had been disturbingly vivid. How could she dream the same dream twice? Now that she thought of it, it seemed that she had dreamed it more than twice, a number of times in fact, jumbled half-remembered images that had not come clear until now. They seemed to hold some significance she should recognize but could not quite grasp. What would the completion of the gesture have been? What would the face behind the mask have looked like, if she had reached out and pulled it off? Part of her reached forward, longing to know; another part of her drew back, with an unease just short of outright fear.

With a little shock Pamela came to herself; she had nearly been sucked back into the dream again. She felt the heat against her skin; her mouth was as dry as if she had swallowed dust. Determinedly she turned over and closed her eyes, pushing the dream from her mind.

Sleep came, but it was not restful. When she woke the next morning she felt sluggish and tired, and a headache sat behind her eyes.

Pamela and her grandfather drove out to the valley in silence. The car bumped down the uneven slope of the valley, the heat rising to meet them. Stepping out into the blaze of the sun, Pamela felt the oppression of the place overtake her, heavy and familiar.

Pamela's grandfather went first to the administrative tent, where he consulted with the paymaster about the payroll that would be given out on Friday. In the middle of their discussion, Dr. Weber's assistant came rushing into the tent in a state of high excitement. Something really significant had been found; it must be seen.

At once Pamela's grandfather left the tent. Pamela followed. A group of men was gathered atop the central hill. They parted to let Pamela and her grandfather through. Dr. Weber and another man were crouched on the ground, discussing something that their backs hid from view. Dr. Weber looked up. His expression was jubilant; his eyes were like gemstones in the brown setting of his face.

"Look at this!" he said, rising to his feet and moving aside so they could see. "A really significant find. And intact, as far as I can make out."

Pamela saw a large clay vase, half in and half out of the soil. It had been brushed clean, and its smooth sides gleamed, reflecting the sunlight. It was incised with a repeating design: Figures of men and birds chased each other around the exposed circumference, emerging from the surrounding earth and diving into it again on the other side. The men wore beaked masks; the birds were in flight, their talons extended as if in search of prey.

Pamela's grandfather knelt and laid his hand gently on the clay. For a moment he did not speak.

"A prize," he said at last. "The man who dug this will have a bonus." He looked up at Dr. Weber, and Pamela saw something like triumph in his face. "Didn't I tell you, Weber? Now do you believe me, that this site will be significant?"

Dr. Weber smiled. "Certainly this vase is significant."

They began to discuss the details of the vase, arguing amicably about its resemblance to designs found at other Mound Culture excavations. Pamela found herself gripped by a strong desire to leave the hill. It was not just the heat, the usual discomfort. There was something about the vase, or its designs, that disturbed her—perhaps it was that the beaked masks were so much like the one she had seen in her dream last night. As often as she tried to avert them, her eyes were drawn back to the incised pattern. Round and round the gleaming clay the men and birds raced, into the earth and out of it again. Pamela felt dizzy, and a little sick. Heatstroke, she thought bemusedly. She must get out of the sun.

She turned and began to cross the uneven earth, stumbling a little as she moved between the hunched diggers, avoiding the tools and sieves and baskets that littered the ground. Sweat ran into her eyes, blinding her. Reaching ground level, she headed for the water tent. Her head throbbed; her feet seemed very far away. Around her the world blazed and simmered. The air was thick and acrid.

Pamela heard distant shouting. The cries rose, accompanied now by a strange rumbling sound. Feeling as if she were underwater, she turned.

She took it all in, an instant of frozen vision: the fallen mule on the rutted road; the workers, their faces twisted in panic; the cart full of earth and stones, its harness traces snapped, gathering speed as it rolled backward down the incline. Like a juggernaut it came, bouncing over rocks, crushing baskets and tools, shedding dirt with every jolt. It drove a tide of men before it. Startled crows flew up like confetti, squawking.

Pamela was paralyzed. She could not move a muscle. The thing was going to hit her, she knew; she watched with a strange clarity as it hurtled toward her. Behind it, straining to outpace it, ran men who would never reach her in time.

And then, seconds before the cart struck, something gripped Pamela and flung her out of the way. There was no arm to pull her, no body to push her—it was her own muscles that propelled her in a great leap to the side. Yet she knew for certain that it had not been she who jumped. Something had jumped for her, inhabiting her limbs just long enough to catapult her out of the path of danger.

Pamela was never sure afterward whether she fainted; she thought she had not. But it felt a bit like returning to consciousness to find herself alive after all, half-sitting and half-lying on the ground, a group of men gathering round her. Their features were drawn with fear. There was a commotion as her grandfather pushed through them, his face ashen. He knelt beside her, putting his hands on her shoulders. She felt them tremble.

"Pamela, are you all right?" he asked over and over in a voice she scarcely recognized. "Does it hurt anywhere? Are you bleeding?"

Miraculously, though her hip and arm were bruised, Pamela was not seriously injured. Having assured himself of that, her grandfather became suddenly, overwhelmingly angry.

"How could something like this happen?" he shouted at the huddled men. "How could you be so careless? She could have been killed! Where's the driver of that cart?"

It was with the greatest difficulty that Dr. Weber, who had followed him, persuaded Pamela's grandfather not to fire the driver outright. The man, his face blank with shock, swore that the traces had been fine the day before. There was no reason for them to snap as they had, without warning. He apologized over and over, almost in tears.

Pamela's grandfather picked her up himself, despite her protests, and carried her to the infirmary tent. Looking across his shoulder she saw that the cart had plowed its way to the opposite end of the dig, demolishing the water tent in its progress, and overturned. It lay on its side, one wheel still spinning slowly. Pamela turned her eyes away, feeling faint again.

The site doctor examined her and pronounced her unhurt. He disinfected several cuts, which stung, and gave her a sip of brandy, which caused her to choke and cough but also made her feel a little better. Then, gently, her grandfather helped her into the car, and they began the drive home.

Pamela leaned her head back against the seat and closed her eyes. She was limp and drained with the aftereffects of shock. What had happened felt unreal, especially the moment when she had been galvanized out of the path of the cart. Already she was no longer certain of what she had experienced, and when she tried to recapture the strange sense of being gripped from outside herself, it slipped away, like the images of her dreams.

About one thing, however, there was no doubt: She had nearly lost her life today. She thought of Elizabeth. If she had obeyed her mother and stayed with her grandfather, this would not have happened.

Pamela opened her eyes and looked at her grandfather.

"Grandfather," she said, "I don't think we should tell Mother what happened today."

He glanced at her. "She has a right to know."

"Yes, but it'd only upset her. And . . . and she'd be angry with me, for going off on my own."

"It wasn't your fault, Pamela. I blame myself. I should have been with you."

"Grandfather . . ." Pamela took a deep breath. "Grandfather, I don't think I should go back to the dig for a while."

There was a pause, and then he nodded. "Yes, perhaps that would be wise. I will miss your company"—he glanced at her, and smiled very slightly—"but I'm sure you will be safer at home. At least until this weather breaks."

"Thank you, Grandfather."

Pamela closed her eyes again, turning her face to the flow of air that filled the car. Relief filled her, cool and light and wonderful. She was free. She would not have to go back to the dig again. She would not have to set her feet on the hills; she would not have to endure the heat and dust and oppression. The memory of horror brushed up her spine, like a cold finger, but she pushed it away. Ahead lay the prospect of quiet days with her mother, her books, and Esther. This alternative, once distasteful, seemed suddenly, profoundly desirable.

Her head against the hot black leather seat, Pamela fell asleep. And this time she did not dream.

Chapter ELEVEN

Two days later Pamela was returning from an errand for Esther, her marketing basket heavy with fresh bread and peaches. She moved along the white-hot sidewalk, hugging the pools of shadow. Hot as it was, it was still nothing near as hot as the dig. She passed the high school, abandoned for the summer.

"Pssst! Hey!"

It brought her up short. She looked around her; the sidewalk was deserted. Uneasily she began to walk on.

"Pssst! Over here!"

This time it was louder. Again she looked carefully around; this time, she could just see someone standing in the school yard, deep in the shadow of the brick school building.

"Who's there?" she called.

"It's me," came the reply, in a voice she did not recognize. "I have something to tell you."

"I don't know you," Pamela said suspiciously. "Who are you?"

"Come here and see."

Caution told Pamela to walk on, but curiosity was stronger. She moved into the school yard, squinting toward whoever it was, still able to make out no more than a dark shape.

"Come on." The voice held mockery. "I won't bite."

Pamela stepped just inside the edge of shadow. Now she was able to see that the speaker was an Indian boy about her own age, tall and well built.

"You're the boy from the site!" she exclaimed.

"You see? You do know me." He smiled, flashing white teeth; it was not, somehow, a friendly smile. "I have a message for you. From a relative."

Pamela frowned. "My grandfather?"

He shook his head.

"My mother?"

He shook his head again, smiling.

"But you said a relative."

"Yes, I did."

He was baiting her, and enjoying it. He was very good-looking, with smooth brown skin and straight, blue black hair, cut shorter than most other Indians Pamela had seen. He was better dressed too, in neat twill pants and a short-sleeved cotton shirt. His feet, however, were bare.

"I don't have any other relatives," Pamela said sharply. "And you wouldn't know them if I did."

The smile disappeared. "You *do* have another relative. Your great-aunt Mirabel. Your *Indian* great-aunt."

"My . . ." Pamela stared at him.

"Don't look so shocked. It's not contagious."

His attitude was beginning to make her angry. "My grandmother's sister, you mean?"

"That's the one." He folded his arms and leaned against the brick wall, staring at Pamela with the same bold gaze he had turned on her that day in the valley. It was the gaze, more than his face, that had caused her to recognize him.

"So what's the message? I don't have all day, you know."

"Mirabel wants you to come visit her. She told me to tell you it was time."

"Time?"

He nodded. "She wants you to come to her house. This afternoon. I'm to take you."

Her great-aunt, Pamela thought—her grandmother's sister. Somehow, from the way her grandfather had spoken, she had assumed Mirabel was dead. But apparently she was not . . . if, that is, this unpleasant, mocking boy was telling the truth. Pamela regarded him warily. She could think of no reason why he should lie. Yet she did not trust him. He was not someone she wanted to follow into the woods. For, she thought, Mirabel must certainly live in the woods. In the Indian settlement. Where Elizabeth had forbidden her to go.

The boy had been watching Pamela while these thoughts flashed through her mind. On his face the look of mockery was now mixed with contempt. You're afraid, his face said, as clear as words. You don't dare.

Pamela lifted her chin.

"I'll think about it," she said.

He looked at her for a moment, and then nodded. "I'll be waiting on the path that leads up to your backyard, if you decide to come. At one o'clock."

He turned and melted away around the corner of the school building. His bare feet made no sound.

Pamela resumed her interrupted journey. How could she go? Elizabeth had forbidden it. Images of snakes and wild dogs and the shabby, rickety Indian village rose up before her inner eye. And yet . . . something in her wanted very much to meet her great-aunt. In all the world, besides her mother and her grandfather, Mirabel was her only living relative.

Pamela felt something stir inside her mind, and realized that she really was thinking of disobeying her mother's order, of following that strange boy into the dangerous woods. Which would be a greater betrayal, she thought, disobeying Elizabeth or refusing her great-aunt's wish? She imagined the look that would spread across the boy's face if she did not come down to the woods this afternoon. It would be contemptuous, knowing. She felt a little jolt of anger. What gave him the right to be so superior?

A dozen times, Pamela made up her mind afresh not to go. Yet each time curiosity reasserted itself. As one o'clock struck, she found herself moving through the house. Almost without volition she crossed the veranda, and descended into the backyard. She walked through the fiery afternoon heat toward the trees at the foot of the garden. Just short of them she stopped. What am I doing here? she thought. All the reasons to turn back rose within her, but something held her where she was. Her mind went blank. A deeper impulse took over. She took a breath and stepped in among the trees.

It was like entering another world. The woods were several degrees cooler than the unprotected garden, and the savage sunlight was reduced to a random stippling of the ground. A little way along the path Pamela saw someone leaning against a tree. It was the boy. He straightened and came toward her. He had changed from his neat pants and shirt to a pair of faded overalls and an old straw hat. He regarded her for a moment, his face unreadable.

He turned and led the way down the path. Heat and drought had worked changes on the forest: The ground was hard and dry, and prematurely fallen leaves lay drifted below the trees. But in the hollows of roots or beside rotting logs there were still flashes of the emerald green of spring, and wildflowers bloomed here and there. The boy showed no discomfort as he strode barefoot over roots and rocks and twigs, never once looking behind him to see if Pamela was following. He set a fast pace that Pamela found difficult to match. Grimly she set herself to keep up.

Sooner than she expected, they reached the Indian settlement. The boy descended the hill, quick and surefooted; Pamela followed more clumsily, her shoes slipping on rocks and dirt.

It looked even worse close up. The rickety houses sagged and leaned, their boards splintered and porches lopsided. Many houses did not have windows; the ones that did had shutters or paper instead of glass. The reddish dirt was packed hard as cement, and dust puffed up under Pamela's feet. There was no green anywhere except for the little garden plots, struggling against the punishing sun, and the forest rising up all around the clearing. A skinny dog panted in the shadow of a rusty oil drum, chickens pecked and squawked from makeshift coops, a few goats were tethered to a fence. Otherwise, no living thing stirred in the quivering heat.

The boy led the way to one of the houses, and Pamela followed on legs grown suddenly weak. The enormity of what she had done in coming here rose before her. The boy mounted the steps and opened the screen door: It gaped into the dark interior like a mouth waiting to suck them in. He watched her challengingly. Steeling herself, Pamela stepped over the threshold. The boy let the door slam behind them.

Inside, the house was just one room, not much bigger than her grandfather's parlor, partitioned at the far end by a half-drawn curtain. The small space was cluttered with furniture: an ancient sofa and chair, a kitchen table with seven mismatched chairs around it, a huge woodstove. A set of shelves held cooking implements, rows of glass canning jars, and a few books. Beyond the curtain, Pamela could see mattresses pushed together on the floor and a cheap scarred bureau. Clothing hung from rows of wooden pegs on the wall. There were two small windows, covered with newspaper—it was folded back to let in a little light, but the corners of the room were lost in sepia-colored dimness. The bare floor was made of wide, splintery planking; the walls were plain boards. Gaps where the wood had shrunk or knots popped out were plugged with newspaper and cloth, but here and there daylight chinked through.

Pamela stood rooted to the spot. Never in her life had she seen or even imagined anything like this. Seven people lived here, in this single room, without a bathroom or electricity or running water.

Despite the breathless heat a fire roared in the woodstove, and pots bubbled and steamed atop it. They were tended by a tall thin woman with black hair in braids down her back. She turned as she heard the door slam. Could this be Mirabel? She looked too young. Pamela felt the boy step up beside her.

"This is my mother," he said. "Mother, this is Pamela."

The woman smiled. She had a thin, angular face, lined with hard work and fatigue.

"My name is Judith." She gestured toward the table, on which stood two tin mugs, as if she had been expecting them. "Come and sit down. You must be thirsty. I'll get you something to drink."

Pamela felt faint at the thought of drinking anything in this place. The boy moved past her on his way to the table. Pamela could not let him see how she felt. She walked over to the table and sat down. The table, at least, was clean. In fact, it was so clean it shone, despite the pits and scars and stains of hard use.

The woman took down a pitcher from a shelf, removed a cloth from its top, and poured a frothy pink liquid into the mugs. The boy lifted his and began to drink; over the rim his eyes watched Pamela. She picked up her cup and raised it to her lips, forcing herself to swallow.

To her surprise, it tasted very much like lemonade, overlaid with an unfamiliar aromatic tartness.

"How do you like it?" said the boy.

"It's good," Pamela said. She took another swallow and set the cup down. Behind the polite words her thoughts circled, conjuring up visions of bad water, strange Indian ingredients that would make her sick. "What is it?"

"Sumac," the woman answered.

"*Poison* sumac?" Pamela looked at her, wide-eyed. The boy smiled ferociously.

"What do you think, we go around eating poison sumac? You must really think we're savages."

"Seth," said the woman gently, reprovingly. "You must not tease Pamela. Of course it's not poison sumac, it's the sumac tree. We crush the berries and add water and honey to make this drink. I'm glad you like it."

In relief Pamela took another swallow. She was recovering from her initial shock, enough to see her surroundings more clearly. Efforts had been made to make the room livable: The shelves were edged with paper cut in little points, the faded upholstery of the sofa and armchair was neatly patched, the jumble of mattresses was covered with handmade quilts. Hot and stuffy as it was, the air smelled pleasant—little bunches of herbs or flowers were hung up on the walls. There were even a few pictures—pages cut from magazines and faded photographs. The whole place was scrupulously clean and neat.

Shouts floated through the air outside; there was the sound of running feet, and a horde of children burst into the house. They were talking loudly in a language that was not English. They saw Pamela and fell silent as if someone had thrown a switch. Wide dark eyes watched her from brown faces. There were four of them, ranging in age from about twelve to about six.

"These are my brothers," Seth said. "William, Gideon, Joseph, and George. This is Pamela."

"Hello," Pamela said.

They stared at her. Their physical resemblance to Seth was strong; all of them wore a less definite version of his suspicious, mocking look.

Judith got to her feet. "Go outside and play, children. I'll bring you something to drink in a little while. There'll be time to meet your cousin later."

Once again Pamela felt her eyes widen. "Cousin?" she said. The woman looked at her.

"Don't you know?" She looked at Seth. "Didn't you tell her?"

He shrugged. "Mirabel will tell her."

"Seth," she reproved again. Then, to Pamela: "My husband is the son of your grandmother's brother. That makes Seth your second cousin."

"Oh," was all Pamela could say. It had not occurred to her that she might have more than one relative here. . . . She glanced at Seth. Her cousin? she thought.

Seth was getting to his feet. "We have to go now, Mother. Mirabel's expecting us."

Pamela rose too. "Thank you for the drink," she said politely.

The woman smiled warmly. She reached out and took Pamela's hand. Her skin felt dry and calloused.

"You're very welcome. I am glad to have you in my house. I hope you'll come visit me again."

"Thank you." Pamela dropped her eyes. For some reason she felt ashamed.

They left the village, following the path into the woods again. Seth walked silently ahead. At last he turned off the main path and struck off down a smaller one. After a few moments the trees thinned. A small clearing lay ahead.

It was a little circle cut into the forest, an island of sun in the midst of shadow. A wooden house stood to one side, with a peaked tin roof, a tin chimney, and a veranda extending across the front. It was built of unfinished boards, its tiny windows covered, like the houses in the Indian village, with paper—yet it was not sagging or dilapidated, but snug and in good repair. Several stoutly built lean-tos and sheds stood at the edges of the clearing. A garden plot, green and thriving despite the drought, offered neat rows to the sun. Chickens scratched in a little coop, two goats were tethered in a shady spot, and a large orange cat watched from the veranda steps.

Seth stopped at the edge of the clearing, so suddenly that Pamela nearly ran into him. For a moment they stood still, just within the shade of the trees, gazing on the peace of this orderly place. The song of the insects rose and fell, waves of sound lapping up against the bright serenity within the circle of the trees. Pamela felt the beating of her heart. Within the clearing, inside that house, Mirabel waited.

Seth turned to Pamela. An odd expression had replaced the hostility.

"We're here." He was half-whispering. "Are you ready?"

Chapter TWELVE

Seth stepped out of the trees, into the full weight of the sun. Pamela followed. They walked across the clearing, up the creaking steps onto the veranda. Seth held the screen door open.

This house, like the other, was a single room, with plank floors and walls and a curtain across the far end to make a bedroom. But the walls had been caulked and sealed, the floor smoothed till it shone. The curtain was a rich deep red, and the mattress lay not on the floor but on a painted iron bedstead, covered by a beautifully handworked quilt.

On the floor and walls were many rugs, woven in harmonious geometric designs and subtle earthy colors; an unfinished rug stood on an upright loom in one corner. Along the back wall extended a series of shelves, holding an incredible profusion of jars, bottles, boxes, containers, bunches of dried flowers and herbs, hanks of dyed yarn, raw wool and cotton, tools, and cooking implements. The only other furnishings were a long oak table with benches on each side, a finely made bentwood rocker, and an enormous woodstove.

In the center of the room a woman waited: Mirabel. She wore a long tiered skirt, each tier a different color, and a man's collarless shirt with the sleeves rolled up. Iron gray braids swung on each side of her face. Her brown feet were bare. Pamela recognized her as the woman she had seen by the side of the road, the woman who had turned to watch the car.

Mirabel stood absolutely still, and the force of her gaze was like a hand that reached out and lifted Pamela's chin. For a long moment she searched Pamela's face, as if she could look beneath the skin to the framework of bone and blood.

Abruptly she nodded once, decisively, and her look became just a look, without unusual force. Pamela felt herself start breathing again, unaware till now that she had stopped.

"Thank you, Seth," Mirabel said. "You can go now."

Involuntarily Pamela turned: Don't leave me alone, she almost said. She saw Seth incline his head to Mirabel in what was almost a bow. The door slammed behind him, loud in the stillness. Pamela took a breath and turned to face Mirabel.

Mirabel was smiling. Her smile crinkled her face into a thousand soft folds and filled it with warmth.

"You don't know how glad I am to see you, Pamela. I've waited for this moment for a long time." She began to move toward the stove. "Sit down at the table, child. I'll make us some tea."

Pamela obeyed, feeling a little as if she were dreaming. She leaned her elbows on the worn tabletop and looked around the cabin, more carefully this time, at the strong colors, the patterns of the rugs, the neat symmetrical arrangement of the objects on the shelves, the pleasing shapes of the few items of furniture. This place was small, without modern comforts, yet there was a wonderful harmony to it. The difference between Mirabel's cabin and Pamela's grandfather's house was like the distance between different eras, but the distance between this cabin and the poor place Pamela had just been seemed equally great.

Mirabel took a jar down from one of her shelves and shook some dried leaves into two tin mugs. She poured water from a steaming kettle and brought the mugs over to the table.

"It's peppermint," she said. "I grow it myself."

Pamela sipped. The taste was familiar: Her mother sometimes gave her mint tea for an upset stomach.

Mirabel was the most Indian-looking person Pamela had ever seen. Her skin was nut brown. Her cheekbones were broad, and her dark, almond-shaped eyes were set deeply beneath a wide brow. Her features were worn by time and weather—and yet there was a vitality in her face a much younger person might have envied, and an upright easy grace informed all her motions. Pamela found herself searching Mirabel's features for some point of recognition: This was her great-aunt, after all, her grandmother's sister. But in Mirabel's face she could find no echo of Elizabeth's, certainly no hint of her own.

"You haven't much of the look of our family," Mirabel said, obviously thinking along the same lines. "You must favor your father."

Elizabeth had often told Pamela this, with approval; Pamela was not sure if that was what she heard in Mirabel's voice.

"But it's there, the family resemblance. In the eyes, a little bit, and around the mouth. You'll be a beautiful woman one day, like your mother."

Pamela felt herself blush. Mirabel laughed kindly.

"Don't be embarrassed, child. I may be old, but I've still got keen eyes, and I know what I see."

"Why didn't my mother ever tell me about you?" Pamela found herself blurting out.

A look of sadness crossed Mirabel's face. "I think Elizabeth wanted to forget me. We had a disagreement about the direction her life should take. We quarreled. She never came to see me after that. I hoped . . . I hoped things had changed, when I heard she had come back. But I guess they haven't."

A disagreement? A quarrel? Pamela's grandfather had said it was he who had ended Elizabeth's relationship with Mirabel.

"Since you're here, Pamela, you can help me with my work this afternoon."

Getting briskly to her feet, Mirabel went to her shelves and began piling hanks of cream-colored yarn into a big basket. She led the way out of the house, and over to one of the open sheds at the side of the yard. Skeins of yarn in a rainbow of colors hung from pegs on one wall.

Beside the shed was a great iron pot suspended from a tripod. Mirabel put her basket on the ground and set a match to the pile of wood and kindling that lay ready underneath the pot. The flames rose quickly; Pamela moved back, but she could still feel the heat against her face. Perspiration was already dampening her dress, and she could see beads of sweat creeping down Mirabel's cheeks.

Inside the pot a dark liquid was rising slowly to a boil. Mirabel stirred it from time to time with a long stick. As the temperature built, the air around the pot took on a heavy quivering opalescence. Within it Mirabel seemed to sway and flicker like a mirage.

"It's blue dye today," she said. "My own recipe. The color comes from blueberries mostly, with tannin for fixing and a few other things. Pass me that basket, Pamela, please."

A pile of sticks inset with hooklike pieces of wood lay near the pot. Mirabel began to thread hanks of yarn on the hooks; each stick held eight hanks. She gestured to Pamela to assist her. When six sticks were threaded, Mirabel lowered them carefully into the pot, resting their ends across the rim. She moved back from the heat and seated herself cross-legged on the ground, motioning Pamela to do the same.

"They stay in there for about ten minutes. Then I hang them in the shed to dry. All my yarn is double-dyed—that way it doesn't fade. See—I did those yesterday. Today I'll give them a second dose."

"And it's just . . . blueberries that makes them that color," Pamela said with wonder, looking at the brilliant hues.

Mirabel smiled. "You can use just about anything for dyeing. Flowers, bark, even stones. I use all the things that live in the woods, one way or another. There's a world out there, beyond houses and comforts and conveniences, a world that's mostly forgotten now. Even we who hold on to the old ways don't do things the way they used to be done. Our ancestors would have used woven baskets for dyeing, not iron cauldrons. But change is part of life. My mother taught me that. And her mother taught her, and her mother taught her, on back for hundreds of years. It's how we Quapaw Indians pass things on—traditions, legends, knowledge, and duty. Through our mothers."

She got to her feet and took her stick, and pushed gently at the yarn in the bubbling dye. Pamela thought about her grandmother, who, for the sake of Pamela's grandfather, had not passed on to Elizabeth the things Mirabel spoke of. Was this the disagreement Elizabeth and Mirabel had had? Had Mirabel wanted Elizabeth to become like her?

Mirabel was lifting sticks out of the pot, holding them carefully so that they dripped onto the ground. The creamy yarn was now a deep purplish blue.

"Carry these into the shed, Pamela, and hang them on the pegs. Be careful you don't get any dye on your clothes."

A little of the blistering heat of the fire radiated from the hanks of wool. Pamela set them on their racks and helped Mirabel thread more sticks and lower them into the pot.

"I had a special reason for calling you here, Pamela," Mirabel said. "Time is getting short."

"Getting short?" Pamela repeated.

"For me to teach you. For you to learn about your people and your heritage. I saw what happened to you at the site two days ago, you know."

Pamela frowned, puzzled. "You mean the runaway cart?"

Mirabel nodded. "It's a bad place, the valley. Bad for everyone, but especially for you."

Pamela felt an eerie chill. "I don't understand."

"There is evil in that valley, Pamela." Mirabel's face was very serious. "For centuries it's been sealed away—but the dig is opening it up again. Our people know this, even if the archaeologists do not. That is why we refuse to work the dig, and why we watch it, every day."

"Oh," said Pamela, understanding. "You're talking about the legends."

Mirabel nodded. "Yes. The legends. Do you know them?"

"My grandfather told me a little. He said they're about someone buried in the hills. But he didn't really explain, not in detail." Pamela hesitated. "He said all Indians believe the legends."

"Many do."

"Do . . . do you?"

Mirabel did not answer. Instead, she got to her feet; it was time to take the yarn from the pot. Together they hung the dripping hanks on their drying pegs. Mirabel wiped her face and neck with a bandanna.

"Hot work, isn't it? If only blueberries grew in winter! We'll start on the second dye now. Bring me those sticks over there."

When the already-dyed wool was bubbling in the cauldron, Pamela and Mirabel sat down on the ground again. Pamela was soaked with sweat, and her hair straggled uncomfortably around her face. Mirabel, though she also perspired, seemed oblivious to the discomfort, or simply to accept it as she accepted the ground she sat on.

"Your grandmother believed them," Mirabel said, as if there had been no pause in the conversation.

"The legends?"

"Yes. We were brought up in this cabin. My mother told us all the Indian stories and traditions, and she showed us all the old skills. But my sister was a restless person. She wasn't satisfied with what lay ahead for her here. She looked around and saw that the white people had big houses and plumbing and electricity and pretty clothes and parties. Beside those things, the traditions she had been brought up with, the duty she was to inherit, seemed like nothing to her. She decided she wanted that world. But in order to get it, she had to stop being Indian.

"So she got a job in one of the big houses, where she could learn white people's manners. She bought white people's clothes, and makeup that made her skin lighter. She wanted a white person's education—she was trying to save enough money to go to college. But then she met your grandfather. He asked her to marry him. She thought she had found the thing that would make her stop being Indian for good. But it didn't work.

"I don't know when she realized she hadn't been able to stop being Indian—maybe it was when your grandfather began to try to excavate the hills, and she came face-to-face with the legends, legends she still believed in her heart. When your grandfather understood, he felt she'd betrayed him. He tried to force her to stop believing. He tried to take her away from Flat Hills. But it was useless. Beliefs aren't like clothes you can take on or off. They're part of you, as deep as your blood."

Like Pamela's grandfather, Mirabel spoke the word with a strange intonation. Dark and complex meanings seemed to hover behind her voice.

"Your grandmother came to know at last that she was in the wrong world. She had made the wrong choice; and because of it she could never return to the woods. That was what killed her in the end—that, and knowing the consequences of her choice. You see, Pamela, she had broken a tradition that had been passed from mother to daughter for centuries. She had cut a thread that should never have been severed. When she set aside her duty, she let evil into all our lives, your grandmother's and your grandfather's and your mother's and mine."

Mirabel stopped speaking. Pamela waited for her to go on, to say what the evil was, what the duty had been. But instead Mirabel rose to her feet again. Carefully she lowered another batch of yarn into the bubbling dye.

Still standing, she turned to look at Pamela. Through the trembling heat-haze, her gaze was like an outstretched hand.

"You have powerful blood in you, child," she said. "Your mother brought you up as if you weren't Indian—she tried to make a choice for you. But no one can make a choice for someone else. I would like you to understand what your mother and grandmother set aside. Will you let me teach you? Will you let me show you your people, and your heritage?"

Mirabel's words stirred Pamela strangely, spreading inside her mind like ripples widening across a pool. They touched a part of her she had not known was there: a part that hungered for knowledge. Before she came here, she had not realized she wanted to know these things. But now, without understanding where it came from, she could feel the desire, alive and vital within her. She nodded.

"Yes," she said. "Yes, I'd like that."

Mirabel's face was grave. "I'd be tricking you, child, if I didn't tell you that this kind of learning is much more than just talking and visiting, like we've been doing today. There's a whole world you must learn. Talking is part of it—there are stories and legends, dozens of them—but doing is the other part. Like the dyeing." She gestured to the indigo yarn, the bubbling dye-pot. "And other things. It won't always be easy."

Pamela opened her mouth to answer. Just for an instant she was gripped by a feeling of irrevocability, of something spinning away out of her reach. She heard her voice, sounding far away.

"I can try."

Chapter THIRTEEN

Mirabel put down the dye-stick and came to sit close to Pamela. "Now I'll tell you a story. Would you like that?"

Pamela nodded.

"I'll tell you how the Quapaw Indians came to live in these woods, more than fifteen generations ago.

"We don't remember where we came from originally, but we do know that the land was fertile and good. There were as many deer as there were ears of corn, and they gave themselves to the people willingly, because they knew that was their purpose on earth—to provide the skin and meat and bones and hooves the people used.

"One day there was a great earthquake. Cracks opened in the ground, all the houses broke into pieces, rocks fell down from the hills, and fire rushed up out of the earth. Many of the people were killed. When the quake was over, the ones who had survived held a council to decide what they should do. They didn't want to stay in that land any longer, for they felt that the earthquake was the sign of the birth of a new spirit, a spirit that hated men. But they didn't know where else to go. The people had lived in that place for longer than they could count.

"The leader of the people was a man named Eater of Distances. That night Eater of Distances went to sleep and in his sleep his dream-totem, the cougar, came to him. Cougar said, 'Eater of Distances, you must leave this place, for there is indeed an evil spirit here. You must travel east. I will be with you as you journey, and I will guide you to your new lands.'

"The next day Eater of Distances called the council together and told them what Cougar had said. They agreed to go east. They gathered what they still possessed, and they began to walk. For days and weeks and months they traveled—who knows, it might even have been for years. Each night Cougar visited Eater of Distances. Each night Eater of Distances asked Cougar, 'Is this the place?' Each night Cougar replied, 'No. You must move still farther east.'

"Well, the people were growing more and more tired of traveling. Every day they asked Eater of Distances if they had reached their new home, and always he had to tell them that they had not. Some of the old men died, and some of the children too. The people were becoming angry. They began to talk about choosing a new leader. Eater of Distances knew he could not make them go much farther.

"They were traveling through a wooded land, with deer and other animals in abundance and many growing things. One night they camped at the edge of a valley. That night Eater of Distances had a dream, but the creature that came to him was not Cougar, but Crow. Crow was not his totem, nor had he ever been a totem of the people, for Crow eats things that are dead.

"Crow said to Eater of Distances in his dream, 'This is good land. If you will take me as your totem you may stay here—you will be lord of this place and of many people. There is great power here.'

"Cougar now came into the dream, and said: 'Do not listen. Crow is an evil totem and wishes to lead you to do evil things. This is not yet your place. Your lands are farther east. You must not stay here.'

"Eater of Distances thought about it. He thought about the deer and the abundance of things growing in this land, about his tired people, about their talk of choosing a new leader. And at last he made his decision. He called Cougar to him and said, 'Cougar, I will take Crow as my totem. Leave now, and never return to me or my people again.' Cougar flexed his long claws and gnashed his fangs and cried: 'Crow and I will fight. If I lose, I will yield my place to him. But if I win, he must be banished from this land forever.'

"So Crow and Cougar fought. They fought long and hard, and many were the black feathers Cougar pulled out with his teeth or slashed with his claws. But Crow's talons were strong, and his beak was sharp. Defeated, Cougar slunk away into the woods.

"The next day Eater of Distances told the people that they had come to the place that was theirs. They were happy, because it was a good place and they could rest. Eater of Distances was happy because he was still the leader. Crow was happy because at last he had become someone's totem. And the valley—the valley was happy too, although the people did not know it then.

"Only Cougar was sad, for he had lost the battle and the door had been opened to great evil. He resolved never to leave the valley. He resolved to stay until someone would take him back as totem, and he could fight and defeat Crow once and for all."

Mirabel stopped speaking. The clearing seemed very quiet without the sound of her voice.

"Is that the end?" Pamela asked.

"No. But it's enough for today."

"Mirabel, what's a totem, exactly?"

"A totem is a guide, a spirit-friend. Your totem comes to you in dreams. It gives you some of its own qualities, but it comes to you in the first place because it recognizes something of itself in you. Every Indian has a totem. Even you, Pamela."

Pamela felt an irrational prickling of her skin. She shook her head. "But it's just a legend," she said. "It's not real."

"There are many kinds of reality, Pamela." Mirabel looked at her gravely. "There is truth in all legends, like the stone inside a peach. A legend tells of real things—it's how we make sure we never forget our history. Eater of Distances was a real person. The journey was a real journey. And Crow and Cougar are real too. Totems are as real as your dreams—the kind of truth that tells itself to your spirit, not your mind."

Pamela looked at Mirabel, troubled. Mirabel might believe the legends, but surely she did not expect Pamela to believe them also. As if she had read Pamela's thoughts, Mirabel reached out and put her hand against Pamela's cheek. Her fingers felt calloused and rough. Her face was kind.

"All this is new to you, Pamela, I know. Don't judge what I tell you just yet. The time for judgment, and for choices, will come later. Then you'll be able to make up your own mind. For now, just listen to what I have to say. All right?"

Pamela nodded. "All right."

"Good." Mirabel smiled. "Soon, I'll tell you the rest of the story, about how our people built the hills in the valley, and why, and what happened because of it."

"The Quapaws built those hills?"

"Yes." Mirabel's expression tightened. "Those hills your grandfather's gutting with his machines and his hired men— we made them. That's not just legend, it's history. History as you would understand it, Pamela."

All of the force had returned to her gaze, and as before, it held Pamela motionless. In Mirabel's face, Pamela could almost see those ancestors, long-dead Quapaws, generations of Indian leaders marching back into the unimaginable past.

Mirabel got to her feet.

"Help me hang up the last batch. Seth will be coming soon to take you home."

Pamela hung the rest of the yarn to dry while Mirabel put out the fire, knocking the glowing coals apart with a stick. Inside the house, she took a pitcher from a shelf and poured water into a mug. Gratefully Pamela drank, and used the damp rag Mirabel offered to wipe the perspiration from her face.

There was the sound of the screen door, and Seth stood on the threshhold. Mirabel reached out and took Pamela's hand.

"Come back soon, Pamela. Seth will bring you whenever you want."

She smiled, all her soft wrinkles creasing, her face filled with an extraordinary warmth. Her hand pressed Pamela's, and Pamela's own fingers tightened in response.

Once again, Seth led the way through the forest, as silent and unfriendly as before. Pamela told herself she did not care. The woods were beautiful, burnished with late afternoon sun, shafts of light stretching through the spaces between the trees like misty golden ribbons. In these woods her Indian ancestors had walked—perhaps along this very trail.

She was not sure when she became aware that a sound had separated itself from the crackle and swish of their footsteps: a rustling noise, as of bushes and leaves swept aside by some heavy, stealthy passage. It was the same sound that had followed her home from her first trek into these woods. All of Elizabeth's warnings came leaping into her mind.

"Seth!" she hissed.

He turned, looking impatient.

"Seth, I hear something. Listen!"

Standing on the path, they strained their ears into the silence. There was nothing to hear anymore—yet this was in itself unnatural. The ubiquitous insect-song had completely ceased.

"What—," Seth began to say, but then suddenly the rustling started again, a little distance away, rapidly approaching, taking on the sound of some large animal loping through the brush. Branches crashed; a wind came out of nowhere. The sounds were upon them now, as if something were about to burst from the trees—and then it was past, receding rapidly, gone. Silence returned. Hesitantly, then more loudly, the insect-song resumed.

Pamela's heart felt as if it would knock out of her chest. She found that she had grabbed hold of Seth's arm with both hands. She released him; the print of her fingers was plain on his brown skin. He was breathing hard, and his eyes were very wide.

"What . . . what was it?" Pamela whispered. "I thought I saw . . . I thought I saw something. . . . "

But what? A flash of tawny fur, a great shadow cutting through the shafts of late afternoon light, something huge. It was so brief, and she had been looking into the sun.

"A dog," Seth said. His voice was hoarse; he swallowed and cleared his throat. "There're packs of wild dogs in these woods. That's what it was."

"It couldn't have been a dog," Pamela objected. "It was too big. It was a . . . a wild animal or something."

"There aren't any wild animals in these woods. Not even deer anymore. They've been hunted out. Come on."

And Seth turned his back again and set off firmly along the path. Pamela hesitated and then followed. It couldn't have been a dog, she thought again. But as the moment receded, she became less sure of what she had seen and heard, or if indeed she had seen anything at all. A dog, she thought, feeling a little foolish. Yet Seth, she could have sworn, had been as frightened as she.

They reached the foot of her grandfather's garden without further incident. Seth stopped, just inside the shelter of the final fringe of trees.

"This is as far as I go," he said. "I'll be here every day at one o'clock—that's when we break for the afternoon. I'll wait for fifteen minutes. If you want to come, meet me here."

"You don't have to come to get me. I know the way now. I can visit Mirabel on my own."

"That's not the way she wants it," he said. "You wouldn't like to meet another dog, would you?"

His dark eyes were fixed on her in that challenging way, and all at once Pamela was angry.

"Why are you so hostile?" she said, putting her fists on her hips. "I can't help it if this is new to me. How would you feel if you were me? Give me some credit for trying."

He looked at her. "I guess I'm not used to talking to white girls," he said at last.

"But I'm not—," Pamela began, and then stopped. She had been going to say she was not white. She stared at Seth; he stared back.

"I have to be going now," he said at last. "One o'clock, remember."

He turned and was gone, moving smoothly into the darkening forest. He did not look back.

Pamela walked slowly through the garden and mounted the stairs to the veranda. She was exhausted, her head clogged with new experiences and ideas, so many things she could not think clearly anymore. At the veranda railing she paused and looked back at the way she had come. The forest rose at the edge of the garden, green and solid, holding at its heart the Indian village, Mirabel, the valley of the hills, the memory of all the long-dead Quapaws who had walked in its paths. Another world, Pamela thought. Looking back, it was difficult to believe she had just been there.

Chapter FOURTEEN

When Pamela woke the next morning, the entire excursion seemed unlikely, as if it was something she had imagined or dreamed. But there were blue dye-marks under her finger-nails; she could still feel Mirabel's hands and see the warmth of her smile. The mysterious cadences of the legend hung in her mind. She found herself wondering what came next, what had happened to Eater of Distances and his people, to Crow and Cougar.

Pamela waited impatiently for the morning to pass. At one o'clock she ran down the garden into the woods, her heart beating. She had to wait a few minutes before Seth materialized on the path, light and shadow moving over him as he walked.

"You're back," he said.

He let her walk beside him this time, setting a pace she could more easily follow. He was as silent as before, and Pamela sensed his wariness, but the hostility seemed to have receded.

Once again, Seth took Pamela to his own house first. He opened the door for her and told her to wait. Then he departed, disappearing into the incandescent sunlight. Pamela sat at the table and drank the sumac drink Judith served her. Judith waited on her, dusting off the chair before Pamela sat in it, pouring Pamela's drink before she poured her own, jumping up to get more when Pamela was finished; Pamela found it a little embarrassing.

Judith told Pamela about her Indian family.

"Your great-grandmother had three children: two daughters, Mirabel and Celie, and a son, Silver Grass. Celie, your grandmother, married your grandfather, and they had only the one child: Elizabeth, your mother. Mirabel married too, but she was never able to have children of her own. And Silver Grass married and had five sons. My husband, John, is the youngest. All of those sons married, and they have . . . Let's see." She thought for a moment, counting on her fingers. "Fourteen children in all. All boys, if you can believe it!"

"So I have fourteen cousins?" Pamela said, bemused.

"More than that, child. These kin-lines are so complicated. My husband and his brothers are your cousins too." Judith smiled. "Don't worry, you'll learn to keep it straight after a while."

"How do *you* keep it straight? How do you remember everything?"

"We put it in stories."

"Like legends?"

"A bit. Not as interesting. It's how we remember things about ourselves."

"Mirabel said that too."

Judith nodded. "Mirabel knows all the legends. She is the Guardian."

"The Guardian?"

Judith looked at Pamela. "Didn't she tell you?"

"No. What does she guard?"

"Well..." Judith seemed suddenly uncertain. "The Guardian ... the Guardian takes care of the people. She helps with medicine, with advice, with decisions that need to be made. She remembers things for us, our history and our legends. And she—" Judith stopped abruptly, pressing her lips together. "She's the person who's in charge. Our leader."

"I always thought chiefs were men."

"No." Judith shook her head, emphatically. "Only women can be Guardian. Women of Mirabel's line. It passes from mother to eldest daughter."

"And my grandmother was the elder?"

Judith nodded.

"So that was what Mirabel meant. She said her sister didn't want to inherit her duty. My grandmother was supposed to be Guardian, wasn't she? But she married my grandfather instead."

Judith nodded again, dropping her eyes. "Mirabel took your grandmother's place. It was hard for Mirabel—she hadn't been prepared, the way Celie had been. But she's a good Guardian. She cares for us. She ... protects us. It's not easy, what Mirabel does for us." Judith looked up again. "But it's not for me to say. She'll tell you herself."

The screen door slammed, and Seth was back.

"We're ready," he said. "Come on, Pamela."

Pamela thanked Judith for the drink and followed Seth outside into the sunlight. A group of young people waited on the hard-baked ground, a little distance away.

Seth introduced them: John, Young John, Charlie, Anna, Margaret, a girl with an Indian name that meant Leaf Dancing, and Seth's brother Gideon, whom Pamela had already met. They ranged in age from about twelve to about sixteen. They regarded Pamela silently, their faces wary. She greeted them all with as much friendliness as she could muster.

"We're going for a swim. There's a water hole a little way off in the woods," Seth told Pamela.

Pamela tried to hide her dismay. She had expected to return to Mirabel today, not to spend time with a group of strangers who seemed as uncomfortable with her as she was with them. Anyway, she had no swimsuit.

They set out, walking in a straggling group toward the woods. Each time they encountered a villager they stopped for Pamela to be introduced, although, after the second or third introduction, it became clear that people already knew who she was. There was a disconcerting sameness in the way the villagers regarded her: a kind of cautious, assessing interest. They had been expecting her, their expressions said; now, seeing her, they were sizing her up. It made her uneasy. She was glad when at last the village fell behind.

Seth led the way, setting the pace. Pamela walked beside him. She could feel the others behind her—she sensed their suspicion, or shyness, or whatever it was. At first it held them silent, but after a little while among the trees they began to talk among themselves. They spoke a kind of patois of the Indian language, mixed with stray English words that popped out of the conversation like pebbles.

The woods through which they were passing were very old. The trunks of the pines were enormous, soaring up toward the metallic summer sky and making a high green ceiling that shut out the fury of the sun. In spite of the drought, wildflowers bloomed, yellow and purple, trembling at the ends of long stems. The air was touched with dampness and the rich compost smell of rotting leaves. The song of the insects pulsed raspingly from every tree, and occasionally Pamela could hear the hollow booming of a woodpecker, or the skitter of small animals in the underbrush.

Before long, these sounds were joined by the rush of falling water. After only another minute or so of walking, they reached the swimming hole. The wide forest stream that fed it was reduced by drought to a rivulet at the center of its bed; where it would have run in wet times were only tumbled rocks, mud baked to iron hardness, and the desiccated remains of waterweed and algae. Even so, a little waterfall cascaded into a smooth bowl of rock, forming a small pool. Tall trees shaded its rim. At its center, the sun struck down into the blue green heart of the water, shimmering.

The others surged past Seth and Pamela and began to shed their clothes, with complete unself-consciousness. In no time they were down to their underwear, and one by one they plunged in. Pamela seated herself by the edge of the pool, taking off her shoes and socks and dipping her feet in the water.

"Aren't you going to swim?" Seth stood behind her; his shadow lay over her shoulder.

Pamela shook her head.

To her surprise, Seth sat down beside her. He rolled up his overall legs, and put his feet in the pool too. The others splashed and shouted. Schools of minnows darted in the clear water, turning and turning again as they were disturbed by the swimmers.

"It's pretty here," Pamela said at last, to break the silence.

"Yes," Seth said. "The water level's usually about two feet higher than this."

"The drought's done a lot of damage, hasn't it?"

Seth nodded. "The old ones say it's the worst they can remember. We won't be getting much from our gardens this year. We count on them to tide us through the winter—we dry and can a lot of what we grow. We can't afford to buy much. We're luckier than some people, though, because our village has a good well."

"Summer never got like this in Connecticut." Pamela heard the wistfulness in her voice. "Everything is different here, even the light."

"I guess you've had a lot to get used to."

Pamela looked at him, but his face held no mockery. He really was good-looking, she thought. And quite nice to talk to, when he was not being challenging.

"Seth," she said, "why are they all so . . . so shy of me?" She gestured toward the others, frolicking in the sun. "And the people I met today—the way they stared at me, I felt like an exhibit at the county fair. It was . . . strange."

He looked at her for a moment. There was a slight crease between his brows. He turned his eyes back to the pool.

"They know who you are. But they also know you were brought up white. They can't see how the two fit together."

Pamela sighed. "I can't win. First white people don't like me because I'm part Indian. Now Indians don't like me be-cause I'm part white."

"It's not that they don't like you. They don't really trust

you. They can't believe someone like you could ever learn the Indian ways."

"How do they know that?" Pamela was stung. "How can they assume things about me without knowing me? That's ... that's prejudice. Just like the girls at school."

Seth turned, with a swiftness that startled her. "What do you know about prejudice? You look white, you grew up white. You might as well *be* white!"

The injustice of this enraged Pamela. "Not as far as everyone else in Flat Hills is concerned! Do you know I have no friends at school? People treat me like I have leprosy. And in case you still think I don't know about prejudice, some of the girls at school took the trouble to explain it to me one day. They told me I didn't belong, because I was Indian. And ... and that I was stupid because I didn't know it."

She stopped. Her voice was shaking. For a moment they faced each other, their gazes locked. Pamela was aware of the happy shouts of the other children, a strange counterpoint to her own feelings. Seth was the first to look away.

"I guess it's hard for you too," he said. In his voice Pamela heard reluctant acknowledgment.

"Thanks for admitting it," she said sarcastically.

He met her eyes again. "It *is* different for you, you know." There was no anger; he sounded as if he really wanted to explain. "You have choices. Your grandfather has money and connections. You can get out of here, go to college, become anything you want. But me—I'm poor. I don't have anyone to help me. I can't change my face or my skin. If you left Flat Hills, no one would know you weren't just like them.

But wherever *I* go, I'll always be an Indian."

Pamela looked at him with the beginnings of understanding. "Is that what you want? To get away? To go to college?"

Seth nodded. "I'm saving up—I figure in a few years I'll have enough. It hasn't been easy. Not many people around here will give an Indian a decent job. I'll say one thing for your grandfather, he pays equal wages. That's why I'm working at the site. No one around here likes it, but that's just too bad. They all want to stay here forever." He gestured toward the splashing swimmers. "Never to change. That's what we're supposed to do, you know. But I want a different life."

Pamela looked at him. His shoulders were hunched; his dark expression spoke of the difficulty of bearing not just the burden of prejudice but the weight of an ambition at odds with others'. Pamela thought of her grandmother, who had also wanted something different. As determined as she had been, she had not been able to escape the traditions into which she had been born. Could Seth?

"What's it like working at the site?" she asked curiously.

"Hard." Seth sounded grim. "I get all the dirtiest jobs. The conditions are terrible. I've had sunstroke, I fell into a hole and wrenched my knee, I nearly sliced my fingers off on some glass that was lying around the mess tent. See?" He held out his hand so Pamela could see the livid scar that ran across his palm. "But I don't care. Nothing's going to drive me away."

"My grandfather said you're the only Indian there."

Seth nodded. "The others . . . well, the legend keeps them away. I expect Mirabel told you."

"You don't believe in the legend?"

He turned to look at her. "Do *you* believe in legends?"

"Well, no. Of course not."

"Then why should I? Just because I'm Indian?"

"I didn't say that!"

He stared at her for a moment, scowling. Then he turned back to the pool and kicked the water with his feet. Bright droplets arced up into the sunlight. "I guess you didn't," he acknowledged.

Silence descended between them. The sounds of the forest rose and fell: Pamela could hear the sigh of leaves, the cool splash of water on rock, the lazy hum of bees and flies, the constant roar of the insect-song. Her moving feet in the cool water created splashes and ripples, exciting the darting schools of minnows. The skin of her feet looked bluish beneath the surface of the pool; beside them, Seth's looked very dark.

The others tired of swimming; they hauled themselves out to sit on the rocks that surrounded the pool. One of the girls—Anna—poked into the pile of clothes and pulled out a paper-wrapped packet, then passed around squares of corn bread. She offered Pamela her share with a small, shy smile. They ate and talked, all in English now; Pamela listened, not joining in, but not exactly excluded, either.

Soon Seth glanced up at the sun. He got to his feet. "It's time for me to go to work."

This announcement was greeted with silence. The others began to get dressed. The boisterous joy of their swimming seemed to have disappeared.

They set off again through the woods. Pamela walked beside Seth, and the others followed, still silent. Abruptly the trees thinned. The valley lay ahead. Pamela and Seth walked to the forest's edge. Only when they stopped and Pamela looked back did she realize that the young people had halted some distance away, as if they did not wish to approach the dig too closely.

Pamela could just see the cloud of ocher dust that hung over the valley and smell the brutal heat. The sky was a curve of incandescent light, the sun a white-hot hammer pounding the earth. Pamela was very glad she was standing in the shade, and that the hills were not visible. Somehow she did not want to see them, stripped and ravaged, rising from the trampled grass.

"Well," Seth said. "Tomorrow at one?"

Pamela nodded. "Will someone take me to Mirabel's?"

"Not today. Mirabel wanted you to spend some time with us. She'll see you tomorrow." He gestured toward the others. "They'll take you home now."

"Oh." Pamela was a little surprised at her disappointment. "Well . . . good-bye."

"Good-bye."

Seth turned and stepped into the sun, moving toward the edge of the valley, where the ground began to dip. For a moment, just about to descend the slope, he hesitated. Then, visibly, he straightened himself and began to walk again, leaning forward a little, like someone pressing against invisible resistance.

Chapter FIFTEEN

For a moment Pamela stood watching the place where Seth had disappeared. There were several crows nearby, midnight black against the parched grass, strutting and pecking and croaking about their business. She had the feeling that Seth had not wanted to return to work; it was as if, at the edge of the valley, he had been seized by the same reluctance that held her motionless within the final fringe of forest and pushed the others into a tight group farther down the path.

Something crackled above Pamela, in the trees. She became aware that the air was filled with a strange rustling sound, like leaves brushing together without wind. She could no longer hear the song of the insects. She looked up.

There were crows above her. Dozens and dozens of crows, ranged along the branches with almost military precision. And not just above her head—Pamela could see their dark shapes in the trees nearby, and in the trees far away—all around the rim of the valley. They shifted from foot to foot, grooming their feathers, pecking the air, croaking. Their beady eyes looked down, bright and malign, as if they were watching her.

Abruptly, like a door opening to some dark place inside her mind, Pamela was filled with terror. Without being aware of turning, she found herself running down the path. Reaching the group of Indians, she stopped. She looked up. The branches held only leaves. She could see no crows at all.

She felt a hand on her arm; it was Anna.

"Why did you run, Pamela?"

Pamela shook her head. The momentary, irrational terror had passed; she felt a little silly. "There are a lot of crows in the trees over there." She pointed. "They startled me."

Anna did not seem surprised. She nodded gravely. "The crows are always here now."

"Where do they come from? Why are there so many of them?"

Anna's dark eyes met Pamela's, unblinking. Pamela felt very odd. A prickling began at the back of her neck and spread down her spine.

"Ask Seth," Anna said at last. "Seth is the one who digs. Ask him about the crows."

They were all looking at her, with a kind of watchful expectancy, as if waiting to see what she would say or do. Pamela shifted her eyes under the pressure of theirs.

"I think I'd better go home now," she said.

Their faces did not change, but something in their regard made Pamela feel she had not given the right response. The group turned and led the way down the path. They were silent at first, but after a while they began to talk, again using their odd patois. Pamela was glad when at last they reached the foot of her grandfather's garden.

"Well," she said, "good-bye."

Unexpectedly Anna smiled. She had a very pretty smile, shy yet hinting a little of mischief. "See you soon," she said.

She turned and ran back the way she had come, followed

by the others. They disappeared quickly among the trees, and the sound of their voices dwindled into the distance.

Pamela watched the empty path for a moment before she turned and made her way up through the garden, into her grandfather's house.

Now Pamela visited the forest almost every afternoon. She crept from the house with stealth and returned with caution, for these hours among the trees were a forbidden secret, never to be revealed. Her grandfather had made clear how he felt about Mirabel and her Indian ways; and she could only imagine how Elizabeth might react if she found out that Pamela was following in her own footsteps.

Seth was always waiting on the path, just inside the first stand of trees. Most days he took Pamela straight to Mirabel's house. Occasionally, when Mirabel was busy elsewhere, he would assemble a group of young people and they would return to the swimming hole. Always, since Seth was at work by the time Pamela had to go home, one of them walked her back to her grandfather's house. Pamela protested that she knew her way by now, but Mirabel insisted: Pamela must always have an escort in the woods.

Mirabel worked harder than anyone Pamela had ever known, laboring from dawn until well past dusk, every day of the week. The number and variety of tasks she performed were mind-boggling: carding and spinning wool and cotton, dyeing yarn and cloth, preserving food, baking bread, preparing and drying herbs and roots and flowers, mixing a variety of medicines and cosmetics from combinations of these plants, weeding and hoeing the garden, skinning and gutting the rabbits and possums caught in her traps, smoking meat, curing hides, chopping wood, gathering kindling, and more. She explained to Pamela that everything she did was part of Indian tradition, ancient lore maintained over the centuries. To know her Indian heritage, Pamela must know these tasks.

And so Pamela found herself doing things she would never have imagined. She spent hours weeding and digging in the blazing sun, till every drop of moisture was wrung from her body and her muscles burned. She followed Mirabel through the woods, a basket of kindling heavy on her back, her hands raw and scraped from picking up and breaking branches. She stirred an iron pot over the fire to make soap, her eyes stinging from the fumes of lye and wood ash. She watched, trying to conquer her squeamishness, as Mirabel deftly peeled the skin from a raccoon or a squirrel, turning it inside out over the animal's head.

Though many of the tasks were hard work, many more were pleasant—like the process of gathering and drying herbs and flowers, or combining fruits and vegetables and seasonings into preserves and relishes. Pamela was beginning to discover a knack for spinning, and Mirabel had promised to teach her how to weave. She especially liked assisting Mirabel with the making of medicines, cosmetics, and dyes; she took pleasure in the feel and scent of the ingredients, the precision of measuring and mixing, the satisfaction of the finished product. Mirabel had recipes for every conceivable kind of tonic, infusion, powder, lozenge, or poultice, all written out in her neat, clear hand.

Pamela liked best of all accompanying Mirabel into the woods to gather the raw materials from which her herbal preparations were made. Mirabel's knowledge of growing things was amazing: From the wilderness of the forest, she could pick out by name nearly every plant and tree. Each of the leaves or barks or blooms or berries or roots Mirabel used had a very specific harvesting method; Pamela spent many hours learning how to cut stems without bruising them, how to peel the inner covering off branches, how to dig carefully so that certain plants could be harvested with their roots intact. Afterward everything was dried according to equally exacting instructions. The results were stored in boxes and canisters and bottles on Mirabel's shelves, labeled in Mirabel's neat writing, ready for use.

Mirabel always talked as she and Pamela labored, a steady stream of pleasant and entertaining words. She had a gift for making things clear, for expressing herself in a way that lent interest to even the most mundane pursuits. Much of what she had to say centered on the specifics of the task on which they were working—but there was more to mastering a task than simply knowing how to do it. To perform it properly, Pamela must also know why each task was necessary, how it had come to be important, and how it had been done in the past.

Mirabel spoke often of patterns. There were patterns in everything: in plants and trees, in the way people lived, in the way they did things, in the past.

"Often the pattern's not visible to your eyes or in your mind, Pamela," she said. "You must let go of the ways you've always looked, the ways you've always thought. Sometimes you can only begin to see if you stop searching."

Everything Mirabel said carried a sense of purpose. She

was not simply talking or explaining—she was teaching, though it was not like any teaching Pamela had experienced. And almost without noticing, Pamela was learning. Her feet moved more easily along the woodland paths; her fingers negotiated more expertly the rhythms of spinning or harvesting; her eyes picked from the green confusion of the forest the plants and trees she had never really seen till now. Right in front of her, the world was changing. She was learning to see it differently.

Sometimes Pamela and Mirabel worked alone; sometimes Anna or Charlie or Leaf Dancing or Seth's brothers would be there too. It was like a party, with everyone sitting around Mirabel's big table, talking and laughing, shelling piles of black-eyed peas or cutting up bushels of fruit or stripping the leaves from plants Mirabel and Pamela had gathered. There would be refreshments—tart sumac drink or a kind of honey-water Mirabel made with honey from her own hives, and delicious cakes or cookies she had baked.

And there would be stories. Mirabel told stories often. Sometimes she would choose the story, sometimes one of the young people would make a request. Frequently the tales were historical: narratives of the southern Indians and their banishment from their lands; of the long marches to a new place in the West; of disease and suffering and treachery; of how the ancestors of the present-day Quapaws had hidden in the forest to avoid deportation and struggled afterward to survive in the face of poverty and prejudice.

Then there were the many fabulous tales of talking animals, demons and shamans, magical events and mystical journeys. Mirabel knew literally hundreds of these legends; if they were written down, Pamela was sure they would fill several volumes. Sometimes they were funny, and everyone would be convulsed with laughter. But often they were frightening. The cold supernatural fingers of Mirabel's narration reached down inside Pamela's mind, and stirred a strange, chilly dread. Perhaps it was the alienness of the legends' setting—very different from any fairy tales Pamela had ever read—or the bizarreness of the beings that populated them—animals that behaved like people, people who became animals or spirits at will. Or perhaps it was the seriousness with which the others listened, as if they were hearing not fantasies but past events that had really occurred.

Listening to Mirabel's stories, Pamela often thought of what Judith had told her, that remembering was part of the duty of the Guardian. But Mirabel was more than her people's tale teller. She was also their teacher, their doctor, their guide, and their leader. Though gentle, and employed with grace and kindness, her authority was absolute. No one would dream of marrying without her approval, or undertaking a change without her permission. The villagers revered her: They stepped out of her path as she walked, rose to give her their chairs if she entered their houses, bowed when entering or leaving her presence. When she spoke, silence fell. When she gave a direction, people ran to carry it out. It almost seemed as if the Indians regarded her as not quite human—or, perhaps, more than human.

Sometimes, indeed, when she gave a decree or delivered an admonishment or told people what was best for them, there was a stern power about her, a sense of authority and force that could be felt. At such times she could be awe-inspiring, like one of the spirits of her stories. With Pamela, however, she never adopted this persona. She was kind, patient, and loving, tolerant of weakness, forgiving of mistakes. She never demanded of Pamela more than she could accomplish, never forced her to do a task beyond her strength, never gave her more teaching than her mind could comfortably hold.

Though sometimes she wondered where it all would lead, Pamela did not question the impulse that brought her each day into the forest. It did occur to her, now and then, how odd it was to find herself here, her muscles aching from outdoor activities, her hands stained from preparing herbal mixtures—she, who had never liked the outdoors all that much, whose greatest exertion had been walking to and from school every day. Yet there was a rightness to it. Pamela felt it every afternoon as she left her grandfather's house, and affirmed it each time she set her feet on the path into the woods. The desire that had stirred within her when she first visited Mirabel, the part of her that wanted to *know*, had not diminished. Day by day, Mirabel led her into that new world of knowing.

Pamela knew she walked a path of Mirabel's devising. For now, that was enough. She was content simply to follow, until she reached its end.

Chapter SIXTEEN

Pamela dreamed again of the masked man and the avenue of torches.

In her dream, the man approached her, the light sliding across his headdress and cloak and breastplate. A little distance away from her he stopped. Extending his arm, he reached out and down, pointing at the earth. The empty sockets of the mask compelled Pamela; with her own eyes she followed the pointing finger. The short grass began to tremble, then to ripple, then to drop away, revealing an inky pit, a shaft of blackness driven into the solid earth. Pamela's gaze was drawn irresistibly down, down into the earth, until the dream disappeared and she woke into the suffocating darkness of her room, her mouth dry and her heart pounding.

Pamela did not understand how a dream could repeat itself like this, over and over. There had been the dream on the hill, the dream the night before her mishap with the cart, and three dreams after that, each one virtually identical. The images seemed disturbingly real, as if they came not from inside her mind but from somewhere out in the forest.

Pamela reported her dream to Mirabel the following afternoon. Mirabel set great store by dreams, as did all the Indians, and dream interpretation was one of her many skills. People often came to her to request an opinion. She would listen and then make a pronouncement: One girl's dream meant a marriage, this woman's dream meant she envied someone else's good fortune, that man's dream meant sickness to come. Mirabel never interpreted Pamela's dreams, however.

"Your dreams aren't like the dreams of my people, Pamela," she said when Pamela asked why. "Your dreams are a bridge, between your world and ours. You can't interpret a bridge."

It was a little frustrating; but after all, Pamela told herself, they were only dreams.

Mirabel listened carefully as Pamela spoke. They were sitting at Mirabel's long table. Mirabel was stripping kernels from cobs of corn she had hung to dry, and Pamela was grinding the kernels in a large coffee grinder, putting the resulting coarse meal in glass jars. Pamela finished her narration, and there was a silence.

"What does it mean?" Pamela asked at last. "Why would I dream about the same person so many times?"

Instead of answering, Mirabel got to her feet.

"It's time I gave you a gift, Pamela."

She went to her shelves and took down a box. Bringing it over to the table, she placed it in front of Pamela.

"This was given to me when I was a little younger than you. I want to give it to you now. Go on—open it."

The box was small, beautifully made of some polished golden wood with a swirling grain. A tiny brass hook held it closed. Pamela reached out and undid the hook and lifted the lid.

Inside, on a bed of dried grass, lay a small round medallion. It was made of greenish metal and strung on a thin leather thong. On it was a raised design of swirling, intersecting lines. Pamela lifted it up. It was light in her hand. As she looked more closely, the sinuous design came clear: the stylized representation of a four-legged animal, with a large head and long tail. She looked at Mirabel.

"It's beautiful."

"It's very old, Pamela. It's been in our family for generations. It has power, the power of all the women of our line who have worn it before you."

"Do you really want to give it to me? I mean, it must be valuable."

Mirabel shook her head. "It isn't gold or silver, only copper. Its value is only for us. Put it on, Pamela."

Pamela slipped the medallion over her head, where it lay, light and cool, just below her collarbone. She put her hand to it, rubbing her fingers across the raised design. It was pleasing to the touch. She smiled at Mirabel.

"Thank you, Mirabel."

"It must be our secret, Pamela. You must keep it hidden."

Pamela nodded. She knew Mirabel meant hidden from Elizabeth. "I will."

"And you must wear it always, even to bed."

"Why?"

"It will help you to fight your dreams."

"Fight my dreams?"

"Yes. Your dreams are becoming more powerful. That's the meaning of the man with the mask. This medallion will give you some of its strength, so you can stand up to him."

Pamela looked at Mirabel doubtfully. Mirabel often said

things like this, things she could not possibly expect Pamela to believe. But before she could reply, Mirabel changed the subject, launching into an explanation of the methods by which the ancient Indians had cultivated flint-kernel maize, the ancestor of this modern corn.

Returning to her grandfather's house, Pamela was very conscious of the medallion, now out of sight beneath the buttoned collar of her blouse. That night, putting on her night-gown, she hesitated, but left the medallion on. Feeling very odd, she turned out the light. She fell asleep almost at once and did not dream at all.

Two days later, Mirabel finally finished the story she had begun during Pamela's first visit to her, the story of Eater of Distances.

Mirabel, Anna, Young John, Leaf Dancing, Seth's brother Gideon, and Pamela had spent several hours digging up goldenseal roots. Seth was with them; he had free time this afternoon because his foreman wanted him to work late that night.

Harvesting the goldenseal was exacting work, and by the time Mirabel judged they had enough, Pamela's back ached from bending over and her fingers hurt from manipulating the sharp digging stick. Mirabel pulled out a flask of water and a packet of little honey-sweetened corn cakes, and shared them out.

"Mirabel, tell us a story," Gideon said.

"All right," Mirabel said. "Which one?"

"The Wolf and the South Wind . . . The Trail of Tears . . .

The Twin Giants," Gideon and Anna and Leaf Dancing suggested. But Mirabel shook her head.

"No, not today. Today I think I'll tell about the building of the hills, and what happened to us because of it." She looked at Pamela. "You remember the story of Eater of Distances?"

Pamela nodded.

"Well, once Eater of Distances accepted Crow as his totem, he and his people began to settle down. They built a village and a meeting hall and a sweat house, all the things they had had in their old home. They made fields and planted crops. They hunted deer and the other game that lived in the woods. They forgot they had wanted to find a new leader, they forgot all the hardships they had endured, and they were grateful to Eater of Distances for bringing them to such a good place.

"Time passed. Slowly, bad things began to happen. Babies died. Game grew scarce, and young men were killed in hunting accidents. Crops were not as abundant as they should have been. And everyone was troubled with evil dreams. The people became worried. Could there be an evil in this good place, they wondered? Could their traveling have made them unclean, or angered some spirit?

"In deep dream-trance, Eater of Distances summoned Crow and said to him: 'Why are these things happening? Is the land against us? Is a spirit angry at us?'

"Crow smiled with his sharp beak and said, 'There is indeed a spirit in this place. It is not angry yet, but it is displeased. It is hungry, and you have not fed it.'

"Eater of Distances said to Crow: 'You told me nothing of

a hungry spirit when I took you as my totem.'

"Crow smiled again. 'Did I not say there was power here, and that it should be yours? If you will treat this spirit properly, it will give you and your people all you desire.'

" 'How must we serve this spirit?' asked Eater of Distances.

" 'You must give it a portion of all you have. It wishes for only a tenth part.'

" 'Very well,' said Eater of Distances. 'I will order my people to set aside a tenth part of all our corn and beans and squash, a tenth part of our bread and pemmican, a tenth part of our skins and weapons, a tenth part of our hunt. Gladly will we do this to please such a powerful spirit.'

"But Crow shook his black-feathered head and clicked his long beak. 'That is not a tenth part of *all* you have. You have also young men and babies, old men and old women, young girls and wives. The spirit must have a tenth part of these also.'

"Eater of Distances drew away from Crow. 'What kind of spirit could ask for this?' he cried.

" 'That is the nature of the spirit that lives in this place,' said Crow. 'If you do not give these things, the spirit will bring disaster down upon you. You will die and your women will be sterile; your crops will fail and the deer will leave these woods.'

"Too late, Eater of Distances saw the truth. He saw that in his eagerness to find a home and in his fear of losing his leadership, he had betrayed not only his true totem but also his people. 'You have tricked me, Crow,' he cried. 'I will no longer have you as my totem. I will take Cougar again. We will not stay in this valley to serve this greedy spirit and go down into evil ways.'

"Crow, seeing that Eater of Distances was determined, flew at him and sank his sharp talons into his breast, so that he gave a great cry and died without ever returning from his dream-trance. Quick as a flash, Crow flew from the dream of Eater of Distances into the dream of his younger son, who lay sleeping in his lodge.

" 'Your father has died in the dream-trance,' Crow said to the son, whose name was Stern Dreamer. 'Your older brother will be made leader unless you take me as your totem now. I am the messenger of the power of this valley. Through me, you will be leader not just of this tribe but of all the tribes that live in these woods.'

"Stern Dreamer, as Crow had known, did not even stop to think. 'I will take you as my totem,' he said. 'I will do whatever must be done to have such power.' His own totem, the barred goose, did not dare to challenge Crow.

"What Crow had promised Stern Dreamer came to pass. The elders of the tribe chose him as leader in his brother's place. Nightly Crow came to Stern Dreamer to tell him what to do to please and feed the spirit of the valley. So hungry for power was Stern Dreamer that he cared nothing for the lives of his people. And though the elders were horrified by the things he asked of them, they saw the power looking out of his eyes, and they dared not refuse. Once again it was as Crow had foretold: Those who escaped sacrifice enjoyed health and plenty beyond their wildest imaginings. And at last, through their greed for these things, the people came to practice the sacrifices with zeal and devotion.

"Stern Dreamer caused the hills to be built, to honor the spirit, and to place himself and his priests apart from the rest of the people. The people built the hills with their bare hands, laboring like slaves; it took five years and many lives to complete them. On the smaller hills Stern Dreamer built lodges for himself, his wives, his children, his aunts and uncles and cousins and advisers, all of his family and hangers-on. On the largest, central hill, Stern Dreamer built a great temple, decorated with all manner of paintings and carvings. In it were storehouses, a mighty stone slab for the sacrifices, and a fabulous stone tablet showing Stern Dreamer himself; Crow, his totem; and many mystic symbols of power. The tablet was enormous: Twenty craftsmen worked for a year to create it. When they were finished, Stern Dreamer caused them all to be sacrificed. It was whispered that the tablet was where he kept his soul.

"The tablet depicted Stern Dreamer in flesh and feature. It was the last time any of the people saw him so. For by his consent to Crow, Stern Dreamer had given the whole of himself to the power; his body was a mirror of the power, his eyes a journey to its very heart. Daily he grew less like a man and more like a spirit. When he appeared before his people he wore a cloak of black feathers that covered him to the ground and a mask shaped like the fierce features of his totem, lest he strike dead all who looked on him.

"Now, the nature of the power was that, of itself, it could only lie sleeping in the earth and in dreams. To wake, it needed the mind of man; only in this way could it emerge hungry into the world of time and distance. Being evil, it fed on evil; in requiring man to do evil to serve it, it corrupted him and increased that on which it could feed. For its food was not really the tenth part of the hunt and the skins and the wives and the babies. It was the part of themselves men used as they sacrificed these things.

"Increase in one thing is often increase in another. The happier the greedy people were to feed the power, the more it had to feed on in them; the more it had to feed on, the greater it grew; the greater it grew, the more it needed food. At first the sacrifices were made yearly. But soon Crow commanded Stern Dreamer to sacrifice twice a year; then four times; then monthly; then weekly; and, in the end, nothing would satisfy the power but daily feeding. To save themselves from extinction, the people were forced to look elsewhere for sacrifices. They went out in war parties against the other tribes, armed not only with weapons but with power. At last Crow's prophecy to Stern Dreamer was complete: The people ruled the tribes to one hundred days' distance from the valley, binding each of these tribes to send a tenth of all they possessed as payment to a power they did not even serve.

"Stern Dreamer had a daughter, Willow Withe, named for the strength and pliancy of the willow twigs the people used to make their baskets. She was the blood of her father's heart, the one human thing he loved; from birth she had been raised so that she could one day take his place and become as he was, the second in a long line of power he desired to create.

"Willow Withe knew her father loved her, but within her, her heart asked: What kind of love was it that gave the thing most loved to be consumed? And she came to see the evil that possessed the people, and the horror of the power's greed. She determined to seek a way to end the nightmare. She began to journey in her sleep, seeking dreams and portents that might tell her what was to be done. One night she heard the cry of the cougar before she slept. In her dream Cougar himself came before her, his coat draggled and the bloody marks of Crow's beak still on him. But his white teeth gleamed, and his long claws were sharp.

" 'Willow Withe,' said Cougar, 'I am the totem your grandfather cast aside. Crow will be totem to your line forever unless the cycle is broken.'

" 'I wish to break it,' replied Willow Withe, 'but I do not know how.'

" 'That knowledge lies within you,' said Cougar. 'I can tell you it is there, but I cannot tell you what it is. With it, you must rise up and overcome your father. I will be your totem, though I can offer you no magic—only the swiftness of my legs, the strength of my paws, and the sharpness of my fangs.'

" 'But women do not have totems,' said Willow Withe.

" 'You will be the first,' replied Cougar. 'And you will not be the last. Take what I offer, and journey within yourself to find the answer.'

"And so Willow Withe reached for Cougar's strength and journeyed deep within herself, searching for the knowledge of which Cougar had told her. For days she lay like one dead, dreaming long dreams. Only the smallest pulse at her throat betrayed the fact that she still lived and kept her people from placing her on the funeral pyre.

"At last Willow Withe woke, thin from her great journey but strong and sure. Like a cat she rose, dressed in her finest clothes, and made her way out of the place where she lived and up to the great temple. Those who saw her said her eyes burned orange, like the eyes of a great beast, and those who watched her enter the temple, where her father was supervising the priests at their daily sacrifice, trembled with the knowledge that something terrible was to occur.

"No one can say, not even the legend, what happened in the temple when Willow Withe confronted her father. But when she emerged, he lay dead on the stone of its floor, and he was once again no more than a man. The power had been set to sleep. Crow had fled, and Cougar was once more totem of the leader of the people.

"Slowly the madness left the people, under the care of Willow Withe. She placed her father's body deep within the hill, in the stone crypt he had used to house the treasures he amassed, and sealed it tight. She released the captive tribes. She caused the temple and all the buildings to be razed to the ground. She caused all her father's treasures to be smashed and broken, even the great stone tablet with its symbols of power. And she caused the earth to be built up above it so that no trace remained. When she was done only the hills were left. She let them stand, so that the people would never forget what had happened in the valley.

"She made the people a new home, not in the valley, but by its side, in the woods. Many wished to leave the valley and the terrible memories of the time of greed and madness. But Willow Withe decreed that the people must stay, and pay for the sin they had committed by guarding the valley and the crypt of Stern Dreamer, and by ensuring that the power never woke. And here we have dwelled ever since."

Chapter SEVENTEEN

The even flow of Mirabel's voice had ceased. Sounds replaced it: the singsong hum of insects, the cry of birds, the formless creaking and whispering of the great forest.

"Do you remember what I told you about the two kinds of truth, Pamela?"

Mirabel's gaze was steady on Pamela's face. The others too were looking at her, silent and unblinking, except for Seth, who stared at the ground.

"Yes," Pamela said. "There's the truth of history, and there's the truth that tells itself to your spirit."

Mirabel nodded; her dark eyes did not waver. "The legend contains both kinds. A truth of the past. And a truth of the future."

The legend had been chilling, like some of the demon-stories; though this tale seemed somehow more immediate, more significant, carrying with it a sense of real horrors in the past. Pamela's grandfather had also spoken of human sacrifice on the hills. Yet that did not explain the way Pamela felt right now, as if a cold hand had laid itself upon the back of her neck. Had it been the way Mirabel told the story? Or the way the others listened? Or perhaps the way they were staring at her now, as if they were strangers, as if they had never seen her before?

"So Stern Dreamer really did all those things?" she said. "He really sacrificed all those people?"

Mirabel nodded. "It is all as the legend tells. Terrible things lie in our past. If we can learn from them, the future will never be as bad. That's why we tell the legend." She leaned forward, her face intent. "But there's more, Pamela. The legend holds the key to a pattern. You must learn to see the pattern whole. As Willow Withe did."

Mirabel's voice resonated oddly. Her black eyes held Pamela's. The faces of the others seemed to echo that forceful gaze. Jumbled images rose up inside Pamela's mind: She saw the ravaged hills, the pristine valley, the flashing fragment she had found, the glowing torches of her dreams, crows perched upon branches, something huge leaping through the underbrush. The sounds of the forest faded. She felt a strange stirring within her, below the level of her conscious mind, down in the place where dreams were born. It expanded within her, gathering itself up—

"It's only a legend," said Seth.

The odd power of the moment was broken. Pamela put her hand to her forehead, feeling a little dizzy. Mirabel turned her eyes to Seth.

"You know better, Seth."

"This is the twentieth century." His voice was defiant. "Things are different now."

"Yes, they are. And our tribe gets smaller every year because of people who think the way you do. But it isn't the world that has changed, only the things in it. The past and the present are more alike than you think. People are driven by the same powers that ruled them a thousand years ago.

You can't change that by saying it isn't so. You can only turn people away from the truth. And if we forget the truth, what will happen to us?"

Seth opened his mouth to respond, but Young John broke in. He was scowling.

"We all know how you feel, Seth. You don't have to tell us."

"I can say what I want." A dark flush had risen in Seth's cheeks. "It's a free country."

"Well, why don't you go live in it then? At least then we won't have to listen to you."

Leaf Dancing put her hand on John's arm. "John, he didn't mean—"

"Don't make excuses for him." John shook her away. "He knows as well as we do what it means to dig the hills. Oh, he talks a good line—he says he doesn't believe in our past, our heritage—but he's lying. Right, Seth? Because if you really didn't believe in it, you wouldn't still be here."

Seth's face showed no emotion; but Pamela sensed his anger. "You don't know why I'm here. You don't know what I believe," he said quietly.

"Stop it, you two." It was Mirabel. "Seth, John's just defending what he believes in. You'd do the same. John, Seth has made his own choice, as we all must. It's Seth who must live with his choice, not you."

Seth got to his feet. He looked at Mirabel. "Don't try that on me," he said, "because it won't work. As for you—" He turned to Young John. "You'll get your wish. I'll be gone sooner than you think. And ten years from now, when I've made something out of my life, and you're still here telling legends and starving through the winter, you remember what I said. Maybe then you'll see where your heritage will get you."

He turned on his heel and walked off into the woods. The trees swallowed him up. Silence spread in his wake. The others stared after him, their faces hard, all except for Leaf Dancing, who looked sad.

"Go after him, Pamela," Mirabel said. "He needs a friend right now."

Pamela got to her feet. All at once she was eager to be away from the little group. She ran along the path until she caught up with Seth. He was walking quickly, his head down.

"Seth, wait!"

He slowed a little so she could match his pace.

"Are you all right?" Pamela ventured.

"I'm okay." Then he shook his head violently. "No, I'm not okay. Sometimes I think they don't live in the real world at all. And they wonder why the whites think we're a bunch of no-good superstitious savages." His voice was bitter. "I used to dream about helping my people. I wanted to show them how to change, so they could live in better houses and not have to go barefoot. But it's hopeless. They don't *want* to change. Now all I want is to get away. The faster the better."

Impulsively Pamela placed her hand on his arm.

"I'm sorry, Seth."

He glanced at her. "It's not your fault. I just wish . . . I just wish they could see I'm trying to make something of myself. If only they'd try to understand."

"I understand. Mirabel understands."

"Mirabel!" He laughed. "Mirabel's the worst of all!"

"Seth, that can't be true. I heard what she said about you making a choice."

Seth stopped walking and turned to face Pamela. "She doesn't understand. She doesn't accept. That's why she told that legend today. That's why she—"

He stopped, biting off his words.

"I thought she told it for me," Pamela said.

"She told it for both of us. She worked it all out—she planned the whole afternoon around it. She does things like that. She . . . arranges things. She sets things up. She makes things happen."

"I don't understand."

Seth took a deep breath. "Pamela, Mirabel is teaching you."

"I know."

"Yes, I know you know, but . . . there's a reason why she does what she does. And you weren't raised the way we were. There's a lot you don't know."

He stopped, as if words had failed him. Pamela shook her head.

"You aren't making any sense. What are you trying to tell me?"

"Just be careful. Don't let Mirabel talk you into anything. Don't do anything you don't want to do."

"Like what? Seth, what are you talking about?"

"Oh . . ." He gestured, defeated. "Never mind. Forget I said anything."

"But—"

"No, Pamela. Just forget it. I let it get to me—this afternoon, what Young John said. I'm just . . . blowing off steam. I didn't mean anything by it." He looked at her, a completely uncharacteristic pleading in his face. "Let it go, all right? Just let it go for now."

For a long moment Pamela stared at him. Then, slowly, she nodded. "All right."

They walked the rest of the way in silence. Seth left her just before they reached the end of the path, turning and melting back into the woods without saying good-bye.

Making her way up toward the house, Pamela felt as if the shadows of the forest had followed her into the sunlight. What an odd afternoon it had been. The legend, the quarrel, Seth's strange half-warning . . . Pamela thought of the dislike in Young John's face, the hostility in his voice. She understood Seth's anger: It must be both painful and humiliating for him to hear such things. Yet it troubled her that he had spoken of Mirabel the way he had. She was certain that Mirabel understood, both Seth's freedom to choose and the unhappiness his choosing might bring. She could not imagine Mirabel ever making anyone do a thing they did not want to do.

Entering the house, Pamela felt the medallion against her skin, safe beneath her blouse. Unconsciously her hand moved to it, and she ran her fingers lightly over the cloth that covered it.

But even the medallion could not soothe the strange uneasiness that would not leave her or shut out the jumbled dreams that filled her sleep that night.

Chapter EIGHTEEN

As August drifted into September, the drought continued. There had been occasional showers and, now and then, a thunderstorm, with great bolts of lightning and shattering thunder. But the showers were too infrequent to do much good, and the ground was baked so hard that the torrents brought by the storms simply ran off into the rivers and creeks, raising their levels briefly but doing little to alleviate the terrible dryness. Crops were ruined: Farmers were harvesting a tenth or less of their usual yield. In the churches people gathered to pray for rain, as they had in ancient times. But no rain came. Each day brought only sun, heat, and dust.

Pamela's grandfather spent nearly all his time at the site, leaving the house at dawn and rarely returning before dark. Often he ate the evening meal with the men at the dig, afterward going directly to his office to attend to his neglected law practice. His cheeks were tanned almost as darkly as Dr. Weber's were—only his forehead, covered by his hat brim, remained pale—and his once well-manicured hands were rough and channeled with the dust of the valley.

On the few occasions he and Dr. Weber took supper at home, they talked less of technical issues than of the problems that still plagued the site. Unceasing illness, injury, and equipment failure had caused the work to fall behind even Dr. Weber's revised schedule. In spite of his best efforts, morale was low. The men were exhausted, discouraged, and quarrelsome. Fights broke out, usually over trivial matters; there had been several near-brawls at local bars after work was done.

Pamela did not enjoy listening to talk of the dig and its troubles. It brought too vividly to mind her own brush with disaster. She much preferred eating in the kitchen with Esther and Sam, as she did most evenings now. Elizabeth had almost entirely ceased to come downstairs. Once in a while she did descend, but only if Pamela was alone.

Elizabeth's behavior had undergone a disturbing change. Since coming to Flat Hills, she had kept herself busy enough, arranging flowers, preparing menus, going over accounts, reading, spending evenings in the parlor with her father. Lately, however, she seemed to have lost interest even in these limited pursuits. Alone in the quiet dimness of her room, she read or worked at her needlepoint; more often she just sat, her hands soft and quiet in her lap, her eyes fixed on empty space. Sometimes, entering the room, Pamela had to speak twice before Elizabeth realized she was there.

Something was not right. It was not just this new inactivity. Elizabeth seemed distant, absorbed, as if she were following some difficult train of thought she could not share. Dark circles under her eyes spoke of disturbed nights. The increasingly prominent bones of her face testified to the weight she was losing. Pamela worried that she was ill. But when asked, Elizabeth simply smiled.

"Don't be silly, darling. I'm perfectly fine. Why on earth should you think I'm sick?"

Pamela felt helpless. Clearly Elizabeth was *not* fine. But what could she do?

One night in early September, Pamela returned from Mirabel's to find her grandfather and Dr. Weber at home, for the first time in a week. From their conversation over the supper table, she gathered that a significant discovery had been made that day—something really momentous—on the central hill. Another vase, she thought to herself, only half-listening. Her mind was occupied with the afternoon just past. Today she had made a medicine all by herself, an infusion of slippery elm. Mirabel had praised the final result.

"We must take care to avoid too many people going down there," her grandfather said. "You and I, of course, your assistants, and one or two others. But we can't have hordes of people tramping around the place. Not until a full photographic survey is made, and all the fragments are cataloged."

Dr. Weber shook his head. "Ordinarily I'd agree. But there's a rumor going around. The men think we've found treasure—the usual unrealistic ideas, gold and silver and jewels, et cetera—and are trying to hide it so they won't get a bonus. It's producing quite a lot of bad feeling, and I want them to see it's not true. I want every worker to go down there tomorrow."

"What an extraordinary thing. Where would a story like that have come from?"

"Who knows? Perhaps you've told them a bit too often that they'll be finding treasures of history. These aren't educated men, you know. Most likely they've forgotten the history and only remember the treasure."

"It seems to me," Pamela's grandfather said, a definite

chill in his voice, "that you are indulging in an overly facile interpretation."

"You know the situation out there. Conditions are bad, morale is bad, tempers are bad." Dr. Weber shrugged. "Anyway, it doesn't matter how the rumor started—what matters is it's there. Talking to the men doesn't seem to help. The only thing that will is if we let them see the crypt for themselves."

Crypt? Pamela was listening now, her attention fully engaged. Had he said *crypt*?

"Very well," Pamela's grandfather said reluctantly. "I can see your point. But we must be very careful. The groups must be small, and they mustn't be allowed to touch anything."

"You hardly need to remind me of that." There was annoyance in Dr. Weber's tone.

"Grandfather." Pamela's voice sounded strange in her own ears. "You found a crypt? A real crypt?"

He looked at her. "Yes, my dear. Haven't you been listening? Today, while I was away in Little Rock."

"But it's really a crypt?" Pamela insisted. "There's really someone buried there? Inside the hill?"

"It's definitely a crypt," Dr. Weber said. "And it's definitely inside the hill. But whether there is a burial is a matter of some doubt."

"I find your pessimism very odd, Weber," Pamela's grandfather said. "There must be a burial. We simply have to find the burial room."

"The absence of grave goods is strong evidence no one was ever actually interred. My belief is that the crypt was never used. It's consistent with everything else we've found."

"You know I don't agree with your theory, Weber." Now Pamela's grandfather was the one who sounded irritated. "It's absurd to imagine that a culture would construct a great ceremonial center, only to destroy it and never rebuild."

They continued to argue, but Pamela was no longer listening. Inside the heat of the summer evening, she felt her heart beating. The images of the legend pressed around her, heavy with the weight of the past. She knew, with a certainty that went beyond rational thought, that what her grandfather and Dr. Weber had found was the crypt of Stern Dreamer.

Dr. Weber stood, leaving his dessert half-finished. "It's time I retired. I have some work to do this evening."

He left the room. Pamela's grandfather folded his napkin and placed it beside his plate.

"Grandfather."

"Yes, Pamela?"

"Are you going to see the crypt tomorrow?"

"Yes, I am."

"Could I come with you?"

"I don't see why not." He offered her his slow smile. "As long as you promise not to go off by yourself. We don't want a repeat of what happened last time."

Pamela shivered a little. "I promise."

"Good. We'll leave . . . Let's see, I think we can go a little later tomorrow, about eight o'clock. No reason to get you up at the crack of dawn."

Upstairs, Pamela pulled back her curtains and opened the window wide. She felt light-headed, breathless, as if there were not enough air in the room. Leaning her head against the woodwork, she gazed out into the night. The sky was sapphire blue, dusted with distant stars. A thousand fireflies danced at the foot of the garden, winking and darting against the inky background of the forest. Not a breeze stirred the heavy atmosphere.

She thought of tomorrow, of returning to the valley. Her throat tightened with a reluctance that was almost fear. But the moment she had understood what her grandfather and Dr. Weber were discussing, she had known what she must do, with an urgency quite outside anything in her experience. She did not question this knowledge or where it would take her; she only knew she must see the crypt for herself.

She put her hand to her collar, touching the medallion beneath it. Inside her mind the legend unreeled silently, a film without a score. She felt suddenly that something was coming, had always been coming. And she was moving to meet it.

Chapter NINETEEN

The car crested the edge of the valley and began to bump down the track, a diver descending to the bottom of a shimmering ocean of heat. Reaching the valley floor, Pamela's grandfather parked in an empty space. Getting out, he opened Pamela's door.

Before her Pamela saw the hills, their surfaces gouged and defiled. The creeping plague of dust spread an ocher stain up the valley's sides. Duplicate mounds of dirt and debris rose along the northern edge. Most of the silvery grass was gone now, worn away by work, and on the bare reddish earth men and vehicles moved like insects, pursuing incomprehensible tasks. The air was cloudy and acrid, thick with the noise of shouting, hammering, truck engines, machinery, all possessed of the strange clarity that sounds held in this place.

It was everything Pamela remembered and worse. Only the urgency that had drawn her here kept her from turning around and running as fast as she could toward the distant greenness of the forest.

Pamela's grandfather led the way toward the tarpaulin under which the long cataloging tables stood. Dr. Weber was seated at a smaller table. He got up as soon as he saw them. He looked tired and harassed.

They exchanged greetings, and then Dr. Weber led the

way out into the sun. They crossed the cement-hard valley floor, dodging trucks and workers. The climb up the hill was rough going: Even Pamela's grandfather showed signs of strain. Pamela panted in his wake, feeling sweat pouring down her cheeks.

On top of the hill, diggers knelt to their work, their backs bowed beneath the hammer of the sun. Dr. Weber led the way between them, toward the western edge of the hill.

About twenty feet from the drop-off point, one area of earth had been cleared more deeply than the surrounding sections. Five large flat flagstones lay uncovered. They were made of some dark smooth stone, fitted together so closely there was barely a chink between them. Where a sixth stone should have been, a rectangle of plywood had been placed.

Dr. Weber motioned to two of the diggers. They straightened obediently, and one removed the plywood while the other hefted a long wooden ladder down into the hole that had been exposed. Once he judged the ladder was secure, Dr. Weber motioned to Pamela and her grandfather.

"Be careful," he cautioned. "It's a long way to the bottom. Jake, steady the ladder."

One of the diggers reached forward and gripped the top. Pamela's grandfather swung himself onto the rungs and began to descend. Pamela watched as he disappeared. Far below, a long shaft of sunlight illuminated a rectangle of packed earth. Cool air flowed up. It smelled damp and ancient, like a basement, or things kept too long in storage.

Pamela's eyes fell on the flagstones. On the bottom left corner of each, something had been incised. She bent to look more closely and felt her breath stop. The inscription was simple, almost crude, but it was unmistakable: a little strutting figure, with wings and claws and a beak. A bird. A crow. Crow.

Dr. Weber spoke from behind her, making her jump. "Go ahead, Pamela. You'll be quite safe if you move slowly. I'll follow you."

Pamela stared down into the crypt. She should not be here, she thought. This was wrong. But the urgency that had drawn her to the valley told her she must finish what she had begun.

Her hands slippery with fear, she grasped the ladder. Rung by rung she moved deeper into the darkness, while the light receded above her. At last her feet touched solid ground. She stepped back and looked up. The opening to the crypt was a rectangle of white-hot sky. Everything else was darkness, thick and inky. It was cold. She shivered, wrapping her arms around herself.

Dr. Weber reached the floor. A lantern was hooked over his arm; he held it up. It cast a yellow glow that feathered away into the surrounding murk, illuminating a large square space lined on all four sides with smooth stone slabs of many different sizes and shapes. They were joined so perfectly that not a space could be seen between them. Four cylindrical stone pillars rose up toward the ceiling, their tops lost in shadow. Other than this the crypt was completely empty.

"Most impressive." Pamela's grandfather was looking around the crypt. His voice echoed strangely against the stone. "Most impressive. Don't you think this stonework is reminiscent of Inca masonry, Weber? See how cleverly the pieces are joined together. It doesn't look as if mortar was used at all."

The two men began to pace around the crypt, their footsteps hollow. The lantern, moving with them, drew tiny flashes of light from the floor. Pamela saw that fragments of rock were scattered over the entire area of the chamber, none much bigger than six inches across. They were of the same mica stone as the piece she had found on top of this very hill—very long ago, it seemed.

One of the fragments lay beside her foot. She stopped and picked it up. It was cold in her hand, heavy, speckled with mica and incised with snaky lines. Pamela tilted it this way and that, watching the points of brilliance ripple across its surface. It looked as if all these shards of stone were part of some larger piece that had been smashed like a china plate.

If all of these bits of stone were part of one thing, Pamela thought, it should be possible to put it together again. She imagined joining shard to shard, like a jigsaw puzzle, matching and completing the snaky lines till one final design emerged.

Dr. Weber's lantern swung, and there was a flash from a fragment to her left. There was something about its shape . . . Surely it matched the piece she held in her hand. She found herself kneeling beside it. She picked it up and very gently touched it to the stone she already held. The jagged edges grated and engaged. Where they met, the seam was nearly invisible. A perfect match.

As if something had joined together in her mind, Pamela understood what it was she held, what it was that lay strewn across the floor: the shattered remains of the great portrait Willow Withe had destroyed. The plaque of Stern Dreamer.

Pamela was gripped by a powerful sense of déjà vu. Surely

she had been here before, gazed on this flashing stone, and touched it with her hands. . . . Another fragment winked at her—it would fit the fragment a few feet away. And just in front of her was a much larger piece, which would match the ones she already held. Everywhere, pieces matched—she could almost see the pattern of joined edges, the incised lines meeting and growing toward their final form—

"What's that you're doing, Pamela?"

It was Dr. Weber. Pamela started, and dropped the stones she held. They thudded on the packed earth of the floor, springing apart.

Dr. Weber stooped to the stones, picking out the fragments Pamela had been holding. He held them together, as she had. Pamela's grandfather had come up beside them. Suddenly his expression changed.

"Of course," he said. He sounded as if he had just made some vital connection. "Of course."

Dr. Weber looked up inquiringly. "What is it?"

"All of these fragments are part of a single tablet."

Pamela stared at him. It was as if he had taken the perception right out of her own mind.

"Do you think so?" Dr. Weber sounded dubious. He glanced around the crypt. "It would have to have been huge."

"I'm certain of it." Pamela's grandfather wore a look of rising excitement; it vibrated in his voice. "Yes, Weber, I'm absolutely certain. Look, it's all the same kind of stone. And see how cleanly the edges are broken. Don't you see, we can put it together again. We can reconstruct it!"

In the coolness of the underground space, Pamela felt herself gripped by a deeper chill. Dr. Weber put down the fragments he held and got to his feet. He was frowning.

"We don't have the facilities for that."

"But don't you see how important reassembling this piece could be? Who knows how much it might reveal about the site? It might tell us more than anything else we've discovered so far."

"Reconstruction isn't practical for us. We have no experts, no protected place to work. The pieces haven't even been cataloged yet—and the catalogers have a huge backlog just now; it'll be several days before they can get to them."

"I'll do it myself. I've done reconstruction in the past. I can catalog the pieces as I work on them. As for a workplace, this crypt is the perfect environment. All I'll need is several large tables."

Dr. Weber shook his head. "There's other work that needs to be done here. We can't have tables blocking access. Look, I understand your excitement, but this isn't our mandate on this dig. We are excavating and cataloging, not restoring and reconstructing! Leave that to the people in Washington."

"May I remind you that I am a free agent. Whatever . . . mandate you may have, I do not share it. All I am asking from you is a few tables. I assure you your work won't be impeded in any way."

Dr. Weber stared at Pamela's grandfather. There was a strange look on his face. "I'm sorry," he said at last. "I really can't allow it."

"Perhaps I haven't made myself completely clear." Pamela's grandfather met Dr. Weber's eyes with a cold, steady gaze. "I would remind you of the fact that I am bearing nearly all the financial burden of this dig. And of the weight my word carries in Flat Hills. And of the fact that if I withdraw my support, you will be shut down."

"You're threatening me?" Dr. Weber's voice was disbelieving.

"I am sorry you don't share my enthusiasm for this project, Weber. But my mind is made up."

There was a silence. There was something wrong here, Pamela thought, something unnatural in her grandfather's sudden determination. The shifting light of the lantern, reflecting from his eyes and casting deep shadows in the folds of his face, made him look strange, unlike himself.

For a moment, Dr. Weber did not speak. But then, quietly, he said: "I can see I have no choice. You'll get what you want. Much good may it do you."

Turning, he headed for the ladder. Pamela's grandfather called after him. "Weber."

Dr. Weber looked back, with a snap of his neck.

"Leave the lantern, please. And see the tables are brought right away. And Weber. I know you're distressed about this. But in a few days you'll see I was right."

Dr. Weber's hands tightened on the ladder, and for a moment Pamela thought he would say something. But he only shrugged, like a man washing his hands of an impossible situation. He placed the lantern on the ground and began to climb toward the outside world.

Pamela's grandfather smiled at her. "I knew he'd see my point of view." He stooped toward the scattered fragments.

Abruptly the darkness closed in on Pamela, the weight of the surrounding earth pressing down. She had to get out of here. The impulse to flee was almost unbearable.

"Grandfather," she said breathlessly. "Grandfather, may I go?"

"What?" He looked up at her, almost as if he had forgotten she was there.

"Can I go now?"

"Yes, yes." His eyes fell again to the floor. He was hunched down, his face close to the lantern, his hands moving among the shards of stone. In the yellow light, his expression was absorbed, intent. "Yes, go."

Pamela emerged into the outer world. The heat struck her like a blow. She stepped away from the ladder, letting the sun banish the unhealthy chill of underground. The relief of being outside, in the light, was overwhelming. She looked behind her, at the darkness at the mouth of the crypt. It had no depth at all; light seemed to bounce back, incapable of penetrating it. The angle of the sun shadowed the little crow carvings at the corners of the flagstones, so that the incised lines stood out sharp and black.

Suddenly it was no longer enough to be out of the crypt. Pamela began to make her way down the hill. The dry air was difficult to breathe, and the burning dome of the sky pressed down tight over the valley. She did not even think of runaway carts or broken axles as, almost running, she crossed the dusty ground. Before her rose the forest, cool and dark, a haven from the sun and the dirt and the dust, from the valley and all that lay within it.

Pamela stopped short at the crest of the valley rim. She had forgotten the crows. There were even more of them than last time: The little expanse of ground between the trees and the valley's edge was black with them, and the branches were loaded with feathered shapes. Never in her life had Pamela seen so many birds in one place. They moved constantly, hopping and circling—a great mass of undulating feathers, pointed beaks, and sharp, beady eyes.

Pamela stood transfixed. This was not right; it was not natural. Why were there so many of them? What were they doing here?

Perhaps she moved suddenly, or some sound from the dig rose up, or a wind passed over the trees. Whatever the reason, all at once there was a tremendous cacophony of croaking, and the crows took flight. They rose up in a great circling cloud. Pamela could actually feel the wind from the thousands of flapping wings. In the air they seemed to coalesce, like ink. Then, as one, the great flock launched itself out over the valley.

Was it just coincidence that Pamela was right in their path? She did not have time to wonder; she screamed and threw herself flat on the ground. The air roared with the crows' passage. The light dimmed, blocked by feathered bodies. In the valley work stopped, as men looked up toward the extraordinary phenomenon passing overhead.

As suddenly as they had risen, they were gone, a great black tide passing swiftly off to the west. The ground was thick with droppings and with dark feathers that had drifted down. The men returned to work again, muttering. Pamela got to her feet. On legs that felt like water, she stumbled into the woods.

That night, Pamela dreamed. Once again she stood on a large flat plane, between a double line of torches. People were gathered on either side. The women wore loose skirts that fell below the knee and great quantities of necklaces and bracelets and arm bands. The men wore short kiltlike garments, laced sandals, and a similar profusion of jewelry; they were tattooed in elaborate designs that swirled over their faces and torsos and gave their features a fierce and dreamlike cast. Women and men alike had long black hair cut in front into squared bangs. All had the sleek look of health and prosperity. They stood together, shifting, whispering, waiting. The heavy air seemed to tremble slightly with the heat from the torches, and with anticipation.

The corridor of torches stretched toward a great structure at the end of the flat plane, dark against the fiery western sunset; at its other end it terminated in an empty sky, in which it was already night. Out of this darkness a procession came, a line of people roped together at the neck. They were emaciated and clad in rags, and their heads had been shaved. They were accompanied by guards carrying long whips, which they used with efficient brutality on those who faltered or stumbled. The captives' bent heads and slow shuffle produced an overwhelming impression of acceptant passivity, as if they were not people at all but cows or sheep.

Pamela moved aside as the procession passed, shrinking against the nearest torch pole, but they did not seem to see her. They approached the building. The heavy double doors were swinging slowly back. A group of men emerged onto the torch-lit steps, wearing white robes and tall feathered headdresses. Just behind them stood the masked man.

The line of captives reached the base of the steps, and the guards forced them to kneel. The whispering had stilled. Pamela could feel the force of the assembled people, each consciousness focused on this place, on the captives and the tall man and the priests. Something seemed to swell, born of all those minds. The tall man held out his arms as if gathering into them all the power his people sent toward him.

There was a stirring among those farthest from the temple; the people were caught by it, their concentration gone. The whispering had revived. Pamela turned and saw a woman advancing across the short grass. She wore a skirt and a tall headdress, and bracelets and necklaces and earrings of gold and copper and ivory and shell. A magnificent feathered cloak hung from her shoulders and trailed the ground. Her long black hair was loose. She was young and very beautiful, and there was purpose and power about her as she walked. Beside her something seemed to move in rhythm with her strides, flickering like a transparent shadow: a great cat with tawny fur and round orange eyes.

Conscious within her dream, Pamela knew what she was dreaming. The masked man was Stern Dreamer. The walking woman was Willow Withe, come to confront her father.

Willow Withe passed Pamela; though she looked straight at Pamela, her eyes registered nothing. She walked steadily toward the temple steps, toward the captives and the guards, the priests and Stern Dreamer. She mounted the steps, her carriage erect and graceful, and stood before her father. For a moment she too seemed carved from stone. Then, slowly, Stern Dreamer moved backward, into the shadow of the temple. Willow Withe followed, and was in turn swallowed up by the darkness within. The great doors swung closed.

The flames of sunset had faded entirely now. The sky was

lightless. The blackness spread, engulfing the building, the whispering mass of people, the passive captives. Now all was dark except for a single shaft of light lancing down like a column, bright as a waterfall. Pamela looked up. Overhead she could see the sky, lapis blue, a square patch framed all around with blackness. It narrowed till it was a ribbon, a sliver, a thread. Darkness descended with an echoing crash. Trapped, trapped; she felt herself expand in rage and panic, seeking release, spreading outward like water or smoke. But she was confined in a small cold space below the earth. She battered against the boundaries of that space, but the boundaries were the earth—they went on and on and did not end.

Abruptly light returned, and Pamela stood again on the flat plane. This time the valley of the hills was as she had first seen it, inviolate and empty. The summer sun poured stupefyingly down, entrapping her in the sticky flood of its heat. Before her stood Stern Dreamer. There was a flash on the ground between them; he stooped and picked something up. He held out his hand. In it lay a fragment of stone: the original fragment she had found. Stern Dreamer looked at her, and Pamela grasped that he wanted her to take the stone, to do something with it. She stretched out her hand. But then she saw that beyond him, crouched on the edge of the flat sunlit hill, was Willow Withe's great tawny cat. Its round eyes, not orange now but russet, like its coat, gazed inscrutably into hers. Pamela froze, poised between two actions.

Without transition, Pamela was awake. She was aware of the heat of her room, the droning insects, the uncomfortable way her bedclothes were twisted around her. It was very dark—too dark, too much like the tactile blackness of her dream. Getting out of bed, she went to the window and pulled back the curtains to let in the moon. A damp breeze lifted her hair. Above the mass of the woods, heat-lightning flickered, as if far away someone was signaling in an unknown code.

Pamela breathed deeply, trying to dispel the dream images. But they clung round her like the heat—almost as if she were still asleep. She knew now that she had been dreaming of Stern Dreamer all along. Long before she knew who he was, long before Mirabel had given him a name, he had entered her sleep. Atop the hill, she had dreamed of him pointing to the ground, and when she woke the fragment was there, the fragment that began it all. In another dream he had pointed again, and a shaft of blackness opened up: his crypt. And just now, he had held out that original fragment of stone. Almost, she had taken it. What would have happened then?

In her mind, Pamela seemed to hear Mirabel's voice. *There is a pattern in everything.* Pattern . . . She thought of the connections she had seemed to see between the broken bits of the plaque that littered the floor of the crypt, of the way the snaky lines had seemed to grow toward a final design. She had the sense that somehow the happenings of this summer were the same, a jigsaw of events scattered across the drought-ridden weeks, waiting for her to pick them up and put them together. . . .

Involuntarily Pamela reached up to touch the medallion at her throat. Her heart was beating; she could hear the dull percussion of her blood. Her skin prickled. She tried to tell herself that these strange thoughts were born of her dream, of the night—but she no longer believed that. Here, alone in the dark, she could no longer deny that something was happening. Some huge process was unfolding. And she, helpless in its grip, hurtled headlong toward an unknown conclusion.

Pamela became aware that there was stealthy movement at the foot of the garden. Something was emerging from the woods, gliding toward the house, dark against the pale moonlit grass. An animal of some kind, Pamela thought, mesmerized. An enormous animal.

The creature raised its head, looking up at the windows of the house. There was a terrible sense of purpose in the way it stood. Its eyes, twin orbs of luminous orange, caught the moon. It was staring directly at Pamela. She saw the peaked ears, the powerful body, the long tail, the short fur. It was a cougar.

Pamela's legs collapsed. She fell to her knees, her eyes still riveted to those of the great beast on the lawn. She was trapped, like the beaten prisoners in her dream. She had never felt such terror in her life.

The cougar broke the gaze; it lowered its great head and melted back toward the forest. Pamela remained where she was, her fingers clutching at the windowsill, her eyes fixed on the empty spot where it had stood.

Chapter TWENTY

The next morning Pamela woke groggy and confused. The vividness of her dream had faded, and her thoughts before the window, the great beast on the lawn, seemed part of her sleep.

Slowly she bathed and dressed. It was difficult to focus on what she was doing. Standing in front of her wardrobe, she could not for the life of her remember what she had planned to get out of it. Making her bed, she found herself unable to recall whether she usually pulled the sheets up over the pillow or folded them down beneath it.

She made her way downstairs, where she picked at her breakfast for a while before abandoning it, mostly uneaten. Esther was concerned.

"I hope you're not sickening for something, child," she said. "You sure look peaked."

Later in the morning Pamela paid her daily visit to her mother. Elizabeth was in her chair, dressed and made up as always, her needlepoint lying in a basket by her feet. When Pamela entered she was staring out the window toward the woods, her hands clasped together in her lap. She looked as if she had not slept at all. Fatigue purpled her eyelids, and beneath the cosmetics her skin seemed sallow and unhealthy.

"Good morning, darling," she said. Pamela sensed effort behind her smile.

"Good morning, Mother." Pamela seated herself on the edge of the bed.

"Did you have a nice day yesterday?" Elizabeth asked.

Usually Pamela made something up, a cover for the reality of her afternoon activities. Lying was not easy, even though Pamela often had the feeling that her mother was barely listening to what she said.

"I went to the site. Grandfather and Dr. Weber have found a . . . a crypt in the central hill."

Elizabeth was looking at her. "A crypt?" she repeated. But the fleeting animation receded almost as it appeared. Elizabeth shook her head. "Actually, darling, I don't really think I want to hear about it. Do you mind?"

"No," said Pamela. She found she did not mind at all.

Elizabeth turned her eyes back toward the woods. Silence fell. Pamela racked her brain for something to say. Inside the room, the dim air sang faintly; outside, the hypnotic insect-song rose and fell.

At last Pamela got to her feet. "Well, I guess I'd better go now," she said.

Elizabeth turned her head. Her eyes were faraway. "All right, darling."

Pamela crossed over to her mother's chair and bent down to kiss Elizabeth's cheek. As she did so, she was conscious of the medallion swinging forward inside her blouse. Reflexively, she put her hand to her collar. With horror she realized that she had forgotten to button it up all the way. As she bent over Elizabeth, the medallion had fallen free.

Pamela straightened, grasping the medallion, trying to hide it. But it was too late. Elizabeth's eyes were fixed on Pamela's hand.

"Put your hand down, Pamela." Her voice was quiet, but behind it something was gathering, like a storm. "Let me see."

Reluctantly Pamela let her arm fall to her side. Elizabeth's gaze was riveted on the medallion. Her dark eyes were like holes in her face. There was a long, silent moment.

"Where did you get it?" Elizabeth asked. Her eyes did not move.

Plausible fictions ran through Pamela's head. She had found it on the street, or in the woods; she had bought it at the five-and-ten store; someone had given it to her. But the look in Elizabeth's eyes told Pamela it would do no good to lie. Pamela took a deep breath.

"Mirabel gave it to me."

Elizabeth's eyelids flicked up. "Mirabel," she said softly. "You've been seeing Mirabel?"

"Yes."

"For how long?"

"About six weeks."

"Why did Mirabel give you that medallion?" Elizabeth's voice was hoarse. Her eyes glittered, and she was breathing hard—but not, it seemed to Pamela, from anger. This was more like fear. "Tell me, Pamela. Why?"

The emotion was contagious. Pamela had to swallow before she could speak.

"She wanted to give me a gift. She said it had been in our

family for generations. She said . . . she said . . ."

"That it was for your dreams?"

Pamela stared at her mother. She felt cold. How did Elizabeth know about the dreams?

"Oh my God." Elizabeth's hands were pressed against her mouth. Above them, her eyes were huge. "Oh my God."

"What is it, Mother?" Pamela was afraid. Last night's dream images crowded round her, dark and fearful. "What's wrong?"

But Elizabeth had lowered her hands. Anger, at last, was dawning in her face. "How dare she?" she said. "You're my daughter. Mine. You're not to be part of that world. I won't let it happen." She got to her feet. "Get your hat, Pamela."

"Why?"

"We're going to pay Mirabel a visit."

Elizabeth dragged Pamela out of the house, her fingers an iron band around Pamela's wrist. Into the woods they went; Elizabeth's feet found the path unerringly, traversing it with the speed of old knowledge. Pamela felt as if she had entered another nightmare, different from the one last night, but equally terrible. What was the horror she had seen in her mother's eyes? How had she known about Pamela's dreams? Something deep within Pamela did not want the answer to these questions. She longed to wrench free and dash for her life through the woods. But somehow she knew, with a sense of inexorability that grew as she stumbled in her mother's wake, that the answers would find her no matter where she went.

They reached Mirabel's clearing, bursting out of the trees into the small peaceful space. The sun fell with terrible weight on their shoulders. Elizabeth dragged Pamela up the steps to the veranda and threw open the door.

Mirabel sat at her loom. She turned her head toward them, completely calm, as if she had been expecting them. There was a silence. Elizabeth had halted, as if she had run into a wall. Her eyes were locked to Mirabel's. Pamela could almost feel the force of the gaze that joined them.

"Well, Elizabeth. It's been a long time." Mirabel's voice was quiet. She got to her feet. "Sit down. I'll make us some tea."

"No." Elizabeth sounded breathless. Her hand was still a vise on Pamela's arm. "I don't want to drink in your house. I've come to claim my daughter back."

"I never tried to take her from you, Elizabeth."

"What do you call it, then?"

"Helping her. Guiding her. Shielding her."

"Helping her? Guiding her?" Elizabeth's voice shook. "Influencing her, you mean! Putting ideas into her head! You had no right. You have no claim on her!"

"It's her lineage that lays the claim, Elizabeth. You saw the medallion. She's been dreaming."

"Because of you! You put the dreams into her head! You put them there!"

"She dreamed before she ever came to me. The process begins of itself, you know that."

"I don't believe in that. It's you. It's all you."

"Don't do this, Elizabeth." Mirabel stepped closer. "Don't deny your blood. You dreamed. You wore the medallion. You spent days in this cabin with me, and I taught you just as I was taught, and my mother before me, and her mother before her. You know how it is for all the women of our line—we all must make the choice. It's in our blood. It's the heritage we carry."

"No," Elizabeth said again. "I don't believe your lies anymore. I stopped believing them when I left you and these horrible woods behind. I shut that part of my life away forever. I never thought of it again."

"Oh, Elizabeth. If that was so, why did you come back to Flat Hills?"

"I had no place else to go! Do you think I would have come back otherwise?"

Mirabel was shaking her head. "You couldn't face the things you dreamed and felt in my cabin, so you told yourself they weren't true. You married and ran away and pretended none of it ever happened. When things went wrong for you, you told yourself it was bad luck that brought you back. But you're a beautiful, accomplished woman—you could have gone anywhere. No, you came back because, hard as you tried, you were never able to let go of the truth. You turned your choice aside all those years ago. You knew you had to pay that debt with your daughter."

"You're wrong," Elizabeth whispered. Her anger had gone; she sounded afraid. "How can you say such things?"

"I know you've sensed the stirring, Elizabeth. You can deny your blood, but it's in you just the same. I know you've felt the evil in the valley."

"No . . . no . . ." Elizabeth had let go of Pamela's wrist; she raised her hands to her face.

"You could have seen what was happening to Pamela. You could have helped her." Mirabel leaned forward. "But instead you made the same choice you made all those years ago, when you left the woods. You turned away. But one of *our* blood can only be given to Cougar or Crow—if she is not she will spend her life like you, belonging to no one, lost and alone. Listen to your inner self—it knows the truth. Your daughter is the last of us. If she does not make the choice, there will be no Guardian when I am dead. And you know what will happen then, Elizabeth. You know what will happen then.''

There was silence. Elizabeth had lowered her hands; she stood rigid, staring at nothing.

"What have I done?" she whispered at last. "What have I done?"

The air inside the cabin seemed thick, difficult to breathe. I'm dreaming, Pamela told herself, but she did not believe it. These were strangers, these two women: one stern and relentless, the other still and stricken. She had been catapulted into another world, a world where nothing at all was familiar.

Chapter TWENTY-ONE

At last Mirabel turned to Pamela. Her face was kind. She held out her hand.

"Come, Pamela. I'll explain everything now."

Like a child, Pamela allowed herself to be led to a chair. Mirabel pushed her gently into it and sat down beside her.

"You must listen to what I say now, Pamela. I know it won't be easy for you. You weren't brought up to our ways, and your mother tried to make you deaf to your blood. So you must listen not just with your ears but with everything inside you. Do you understand?"

"I think so," Pamela whispered.

"You must remember all I've told you, about truth and dreaming, about legends, about the patterns that are in everything."

Pamela nodded.

"Good. Listen now. When Willow Withe killed the body of her father, she also tried to kill his spirit and the power that owned it. But they were too strong. She could only set them to sleep. It was a very deep sleep, but even the soundest sleepers can be awakened. So she took upon herself the task of seeing that Stern Dreamer never woke again. She became the first Guardian of our people. Since her time there has always been a Guardian. Guardianship is passed from mother to eldest daughter. For more than five centuries this was an unbroken line.

"But when it came time for my sister to become Guardian, she chose to reject her heritage. And so the Guardianship came to me. There was still a Guardian, and Stern Dreamer still slept, but the line of succession had been broken. Some of the binding power had been lost. Some of Stern Dreamer's evil was released into the world.

"It blighted all of us. It made me childless. It destroyed my sister's marriage. It let hate into her heart and the heart of your grandfather. They might have survived the hate of others, but against the hatred within, they were powerless. My sister realized this in the end, but it was too late.

"Before my sister died, I took Elizabeth and began to teach her. For a while I thought I would be successful, and that the break would be healed."

Mirabel glanced at Elizabeth, still standing stiff and waxen by the door. Her face was fixed, as if she did not hear what was being said.

"But the evil that blighted her parents' lives blighted hers too. She was not strong enough to face it. In the end, she rejected Guardianship and ran away from Flat Hills. The line of succession was broken a second time. For a second time I was forced to accept a Guardianship that was not rightfully mine. Still more of the binding power was lost. Stern Dreamer began to stir in his sleep.

"While I'm Guardian, he can never waken fully. But he is closer to consciousness than he has been since the time of Willow Withe. He's strong enough now to reach out and touch the living—to send dreams, to wither crops, to cause pregnant women to abort, to sicken children and animals. These haven't been good years for us, since Elizabeth left.

"And now, once again, the time for succession is coming. It's your time, Pamela. You're the eldest daughter of the eldest daughter of my sister. You're the one who must be the next Guardian."

She was looking into Pamela's eyes, with that intense gaze that pulled at Pamela's soul. Pamela stared back, mesmerized. Mirabel's face seemed to float on the dim air, as if in a dream. She *was* dreaming, she thought. This could not possibly be real.

"It's your dreams that signal the time for succession," Mirabel continued. "Each Guardian is the descendant of Willow Withe, but she is also the descendant of Stern Dreamer. Each Guardian must fight the battle Willow Withe fought and set Stern Dreamer to sleep within herself, as Willow Withe set him to sleep within the earth. Otherwise Stern Dreamer will possess her and through her come to wakefulness again. Guardians are trained from babyhood in preparation for this battle.

"For you, Pamela, the dreams hold a special danger. Stern Dreamer is more powerful now than he has been in centuries. And you're untrained, unprepared. Because of these things, he can reach you in a way he's never been able to reach the other Guardians. That's what happened on the hill the first time you went to the valley. He recognized you when you lay down to sleep, and he sent you the stone fragment. You gave it to your grandfather, and he caused the hills to be opened. The deeper they dig—the closer they come to his resting place—the stronger he becomes. And every time you dream, he struggles to get hold of you, to win you for himself. You must fight your battle soon, or you'll never be able to fight it at all. He'll be too powerful to defeat."

Mirabel leaned forward. Her dark eyes were like bottomless pools.

"You're the last of us, Pamela. There are no more daughters of Willow Withe's line. If you fail the test or lose the battle or run away as your mother did, there'll be no one left to guard once I'm gone. Either way, Stern Dreamer wins. He will lose only if you fight him and set him fully to sleep again. This is your heritage, Pamela, it's what you were born for. You must heal the break my sister made. You must carry on our line."

Mirabel stopped. She seemed to be waiting. Pamela had no idea how to respond. I'm dreaming, she kept thinking, over and over. I'm dreaming.

"Pamela." Mirabel gave her a little shake. "Pamela, have you understood what I've told you?"

With difficulty, Pamela focused her eyes. Mirabel's face seemed blurred; the cabin had grown very dim.

"This can't be true," she said through stiff lips. "All of that—it's a . . . a myth, a fairy tale. Dead people can't reach out and touch the living. Why are you telling me this?"

Very gently, Mirabel took both Pamela's hands. Her fingers were rough and warm. "I know this is very difficult for you to accept. But it is true. Remember the two truths—the truth of the words and the truth beneath them. Look beneath my words. You can do it if you'll let yourself."

Pamela pulled her hands away. She shook her head.

"Think of your dreams, Pamela. You can't deny your

dreams. And your totem—you've seen your totem. You and Seth—remember? Look for the pattern."

Pattern. And suddenly Pamela stood before her window again, the fragments of Stern Dreamer's plaque glittering in her mind's eye, a great cat prowling the night-bound lawn outside. As she had then, she felt herself on the edge of understanding, all the pieces of what had happened to her since she came to Flat Hills spreading out before her, ready to join together. Terror clutched at her. She did not want to understand. She pushed away from Mirabel and ran over to where Elizabeth stood, a beautiful, gaunt statue.

"Mother," she cried urgently. "Mother, say it isn't true. Tell me it's all a story. Tell me!"

Elizabeth's eyes turned toward her. She did not move. In her face Pamela saw the answer. She started away.

"You never told me the truth!" Pamela heard her own voice, ragged and desperate. "Never once, from the beginning!"

Elizabeth held out her hand, as if begging Pamela to stop. "I wanted to keep you safe. I thought if you never knew . . ."

"But *you* knew! How could you bring me here, when you knew? How could you not warn me? Why didn't you help me?"

"No, Pamela." Elizabeth had begun to weep; Pamela saw the tears on her cheeks. "You don't understand. I had to come back. We had no money, no prospects. I never thought this could happen to you, please believe me. I never thought you could be affected. You're three-quarters white! I thought that blood would be stronger—"

"No." It was Mirabel. "Blood calls to blood. The break

tries to heal itself. Life is all choice—but in this one thing, neither of you has any choice at all. You cannot lose your blood. You can't pretend it away."

Elizabeth looked at Mirabel, the tears running freely now. "Can't you stop it?" she appealed. "Can't you make it go away, at least till she's stronger?"

Mirabel shook her head. "It chooses its own time. I'll protect her as much as I can. I'll shield her, and I'll help her. But she must fight this battle alone. As I did."

"I'll do it!" Elizabeth cried. "Let me do it, the way I should have done years ago—just let it not be Pamela!"

"It's too late, Elizabeth. You've already chosen. You can't unmake your choice."

Pamela could bear no more. The dark air of the cabin was suffocating her; she felt its walls closing in. She must get out. Out into the light and air, away from Elizabeth with her tears and Mirabel with her stories. She pushed past her mother, out the door, into the clearing and the cruel sun. Vaguely she heard their voices calling after her, but then she entered the forest and all sounds were lost except for her running feet and panting breath.

She did not consciously realize where she was heading until she arrived at the Indian settlement; she knew then she was looking for Seth. Rational, levelheaded Seth, who did not believe the legend.

She pounded across the baked clay and wrenched open the door to his house. Judith, startled, looked up from the woodstove. Two of Seth's brothers were sitting at the table. They stared at Pamela with their black eyes.

"I'm looking for Seth," Pamela gasped out. "Is he here?"

"No, he's over at the swimming hole. Pamela, what's wrong? Pamela—"

But Pamela was gone, running through the village toward the path that led to the swimming hole. She felt eyes on her, the eyes of the people who sat on their porches, the eyes of the people who came out to watch her fly past. They knew—they had known all along. That was why they had gazed at her so strangely when she first came here. If she were to look up at them, she would see Mirabel's eyes in every face.

Gideon and Anna were at the swimming hole along with Seth, sitting in the shade at the water's edge. They stared at her as she burst from the trees. They knew too—she remembered their faces that day in the woods, when she had first noticed the crows. She clutched at Seth's arm.

"Seth . . . I have to talk to you. Alone. Please."

He looked at her, puzzled, but got to his feet and followed her a little distance into the trees. She blurted out what had happened, a great rush of breathless words.

"It isn't true, is it, Seth?" she finished. "It's not real. There isn't any power. I don't have to fight any battles. I don't have to be the Guardian. Tell me, Seth. Tell me it's not real."

He reached out to her, a dark and complex expression on his face. He touched her arm briefly and drew back his hand. His eyes shifted away from her desperate gaze.

"I can't tell you that, Pamela. Not exactly."

Pamela stared at him. "You . . . you believe it too, don't you?" she said. "After everything you told me. You believe the legend too."

"No," he said. "No, Pamela, you don't understand."

But Pamela could see the fear in his eyes, and the weakness of his voice replied more truly than his words. She felt a terrible despair. There was no one now who could tell her what she wished to hear.

"You lied to me!" she accused. "Just like my mother. Just like Mirabel. All of you knew, but you never said anything!"

"I tried to warn you—"

"No, no! You never explained!"

"Pamela, you'd never have believed me. And . . . and I thought you'd be all right. You're not from our world. I thought that would keep you safe."

"Well, it hasn't! It hasn't! Oh, God!" Pamela was crying now, tears streaming down her cheeks. "Why is this happening to me? I don't want it! I don't want it!"

"Pamela, please." He was pleading. "You have to understand. The legend is only as powerful as you let it be. I . . . I do believe it *used* to be true—a long time ago, centuries ago. But the world is different now. Those things don't make sense anymore. We have to let them go. We can choose not to believe. Don't you see, Pamela, if you don't let the legend get hold of you, it has no power."

But Pamela knew his words were lies. She had never believed in the legend at all, but it had caught her anyway, and now it wrapped her up so tightly she could not see how to get free. From the depths of her own desperation and despair, she struck out at Seth.

"You say you don't believe it, but you do. You're like the others after all. You'll never leave Flat Hills. You'll stay here until you rot. It's all talk, all that stuff about not believing, about getting away. All talk!"

She hurled the words at him as if she could shatter the

terrible grip of Mirabel's revelations. His face became very still.

"At least I know what I want," he said. "You're yelling at me for believing in the legend. But all the time *you* believe it yourself. If you didn't, you wouldn't be so upset. Have you thought about that? Pamela—"

But Pamela ignored his outstretched hand. She turned and ran stumbling through the forest. Her legs felt limp and weak, her breath burned in her chest—but still she ran, as if she were trying to outdistance the terrible fear that gripped her. It kept pace, breathing at her back like a cold wind, a hideous dream from which she could not awaken.

At last she was forced to stop. Panting, she stood on the path in a part of the forest she did not recognize. Gradually her breath quieted. She heard the roar of insects, the sigh of wind, the brush of leaf on leaf, all the sound and multiplicity of the great forest.

And, far away among the trees, something else. A rustling, rising louder as it approached, rolling toward her like the sound of great running feet. Was it real? Was she imagining it? Bursting on her mind's eye came the vision of a tawny beast, leaping through the underbrush, standing still and purposeful on a moonlit lawn. Naked terror overwhelmed her. She whirled and fled.

Chapter TWENTY-TWO

When Pamela returned to her grandfather's house that afternoon, dirty and disheveled and scratched, her face salty with tears and sweat, she ran up the stairs to her room and flung herself on her bed. There she wept for what seemed like hours, unable to control the sobbing that racked her body. She cried for herself, for her fear, for all the things she did not understand, for the betrayals of those she had thought closest to her.

At last, exhausted, she fell asleep. She woke that evening, the twilit sky glowing dully outside her windows. She felt calm now, the kind of calm that comes when all hope is gone. While she slept, the puzzle pieces had cemented themselves together. Her waking mind now saw the picture whole, its various parts joined so closely together that no room was left for denial. However she might struggle against the fate that claimed her, she knew that what Mirabel had told her was true. She had known it in Mirabel's cabin; she had known it, without understanding, as she knelt before her window the night before.

And now she, a sixteen-year-old girl, must wage a terrible battle—a battle whose nature she did not understand, much less how it must be fought. If she lost, an inconceivable horror would be loosed into the world. If, against all odds, she was successful, she must then become Guardian of an entire Indian tribe. Either result seemed equally impossible. Where would she find the ability to do what must be done? Where would she find the skill to fight, the strength to bear whatever came later?

Pamela rolled over and buried her face in the pillow. Her fragile calm trembled. If only Elizabeth had not come back to Arkansas. If only Pamela had not gone to the hills—or, going, had not lain down to sleep. If only she had left the fragment where it was, giving her grandfather no evidence with which to start the dig. If only she had not gone with Seth that day. If only she had never seen Mirabel, never walked the woods. If only . . . If only . . .

Pamela pushed back the threatening tears—she did not want to cry anymore. It would not have mattered. All this would have found a way to happen regardless. This story was much older than Pamela; it was not about her alone. She was only the final link in a chain of events that had begun to unfold well before her birth and would go on unfolding no matter what she did or did not do.

It would come, this battle of which Mirabel had spoken, this moment of choice; it would come as inevitably as the night, as the rising sun, as dreams. Ready or not, Pamela must face it. There was nothing she could do.

Except wait.

Elizabeth returned to the house sometime during the night, in a state of utter collapse. Esther found her in the morning, slumped against the veranda railing as if she had been too weary to go farther. Her eyes were open, but she seemed unconscious: She did not respond to the flame the doctor held before her face, nor did she answer when spoken to, nor did she seem in any way aware of what was going on around her. The doctor diagnosed a nervous breakdown and ordered complete rest.

Esther put Elizabeth to bed and cared for her as if she were a baby. Pamela went daily to sit beside her mother. Elizabeth's face was still and waxen, the face of a mannequin; the only sign of life was the occasional flutter of her eyelids, the slight motion of her breathing. It was as if she had gone away, drawing her consciousness down to some still point deep inside herself.

Pamela understood that this was her mother's way of coping. Elizabeth had never been able to prevent herself from understanding the truth, and yet, just as certainly, she had never been able to face it. Between the two extremes she had been paralyzed. Now, just as Pamela, knowing the truth, had chosen to wait, Elizabeth, also knowing it, had chosen not to.

Waiting was not easy. Rather than sit idly, Pamela resumed the activities she had pursued before the afternoons with Mirabel, before the dig: She helped Esther around the house, she read, she listened to the radio, she worked in the garden with Sam. She no longer went to the woods. She did not want to see Mirabel, or Seth either, though when she allowed herself to think about it she was aware that she missed them both more than she would have expected.

But her composure was the sort of brittle quietude that might be felt by someone diagnosed with a dreadful disease, who waited for an operation that might or might not cure it.

Beneath every moment lay a great well of panic. Occasionally, without warning, the panic would break through, and Pamela would feel the full force of the thing she waited for, approaching in real time as Stern Dreamer had approached in sleep. It must reach her soon. How would she know? she asked herself again and again. How would she recognize when it was time?

The nights were most difficult. She desperately feared her dreams, and she lay awake as long as she possibly could, resisting sleep until it took her by force. But perhaps it was her own willpower; perhaps it was the medallion; perhaps Stern Dreamer had done all he could through Pamela's sleep and no longer needed to reach out to her. Whatever the reason, there were no more dreams.

A week after the confrontation with Mirabel, Pamela returned to school. She barely noticed the eyes that followed her as she walked through the school yard. She did not care that in her classroom she was the only one without a deskmate.

To Pamela's surprise, the teacher began the class by talking about the dig and its progress over the summer, dwelling upon the sudden prosperity it had brought to Flat Hills.

"We have a girl in our class who can give us an inside view of the excavation process," the teacher said. "Her grandfather is responsible for bringing the dig to Flat Hills, and I believe she's been there a number of times. Pamela, would you like to come up here and tell us something about what you've seen?"

For a moment Pamela was paralyzed by the sheer unexpectedness of it. Heads had turned as the teacher spoke; now every eye in the room was fixed on her. She forced herself to rise, to walk slowly to the front of the room, to face her classmates. Her throat was dry as dust.

"Go on, Pamela," the teacher said encouragingly. "We're all very interested."

Stumbling, Pamela began to speak. She talked about the process of excavation, about the cataloging and mapping, about what had been found—the pottery shards, the arrowheads and spearheads, the vases, the jewelry. The eyes of her classmates did not waver. She felt more and more awkward as she continued, conscious of the subtext that ran darkly beneath her words: the heat, the dust, the accidents and injuries, the crows, the legends, the crypt. She could not bring herself to talk about the crypt.

At last she could think of no more to say. She looked at the teacher, who smiled at her.

"Thank you, Pamela, that was very interesting. Now, I'm sure many of you have questions you'd like to ask."

There was some fidgeting and muttering. Then one of the boys raised his hand.

"My pa's been working out there. He says they found some kind of hole in the ground, some kind of tomb or something. He says it was full of gold and silver and stuff."

He waited for an answer. The others were waiting too; Pamela could feel their attention focused on her.

"They did find a tomb. A crypt. But it was empty." For an instant, mica seemed to flash at the corners of Pamela's eyes. "I . . . I saw it myself."

"Yeah, my pa saw it too," the boy said. "He says the

same—there wasn't nothing there except for some rocks around the floor. But my pa says that's because all the good stuff got hid before they took the workmen down."

"That's right," affirmed a girl at the back of the room. "They're only pretending to find rocks and stuff. Really they're finding valuable things. That's what my dad says. And he should know—he works in the cook tent, and he hears everyone talking."

"My cousin says his friend told him he saw a silver necklace," another girl said. "It was on one of the tables where they put things they find. His friend said it was there one minute, then it was gone, and no one knew where it went."

One after another they spoke up. More than half the students in the class had fathers or brothers or other relatives who worked at the site. All of them had some tale of valuables found but denied, of treasures uncovered but whisked away. No one had actually seen these fabulous items—but they had heard of them, or they knew someone who said they had seen them. Pamela listened, shaking her head, to this outpouring of gossip and rumor.

"None of that is true," she said at last. "All they've found is what I told you. Really. All the stories about treasure are just rumors. They haven't found anything like that."

"That's what *you* say," said the boy who had spoken first. His eyes were hard.

"My grandfather and Dr. Weber talk about it every day at supper," Pamela said defensively. "I've been to the site myself. I'd know if they'd found anything like that."

"Yeah, but you wouldn't tell us. It's your grandfather who

runs the show. He's always lived off other people. He's always made money off our sweat. Why should this be any different?''

Pamela was speechless. The class was silent, every eye turned on her. In their faces she read an implacable hostility, a set antagonism utterly different from the offhand contempt with which she had been regarded before. Desperately she tried to think of some way to convince them of their error, to prove to them she was not lying. But the words dried in her mouth. She knew they would not believe her.

The teacher, belatedly sensing the tension that filled the room, dismissed Pamela back to her seat and changed the subject. The dig was not mentioned again.

Pamela passed the rest of the day in a daze. She had not thought she could care; she had not thought anything could be worse than the prejudice of last year. She had been wrong. It seemed to her that in every facet of her life she was caught between impossible extremes.

Walking home alone, she thought of Dr. Weber, showing the crypt to the workmen in an effort to defuse the rumor. Did he know his efforts had not succeeded? Did he know how strong the rumor had become?

About a week after school started, Pamela's grandfather appeared for supper. Since the discovery of the crypt he had been leaving for the site at dawn and returning late at night, after Pamela was in bed. She had not seen him for many days.

Sitting across from him at the dining table, Pamela was shocked at his appearance. His face was haggard beneath its tan; his usually impeccably groomed hair was untidy. Dark circles underlined his eyes, as if he had not slept. And he had lost weight. Surely the skin had not hung so loosely from his jaw and cheekbones two weeks ago. He ate in silence, slowly and without enjoyment. His hands trembled slightly, so that his fork and knife occasionally clattered against the plate.

About halfway through the meal, Pamela heard the sound of the front door opening. There were quick footsteps in the parlor. Dr. Weber appeared. His face was flushed, and his blue-green eyes seemed very brilliant.

"Do you know what happened today?" he demanded. Pamela's grandfather looked at him, his fork poised in midair.

"I have been away today on business," he said. "I haven't had a chance to visit the dig."

"Well, I'll tell you, then." There was anger in Dr. Weber's voice. "Henry Wallis fell into the crypt. I've just come from the hospital."

Pamela's grandfather leaned forward. "My mosaic," he said in a tense voice. "Was it damaged?"

Dr. Weber stared at him. "Don't you want to know how Henry is?"

"Of course. Of course. Not seriously injured, I hope?"

"More seriously than your mosaic. He's dead."

There was a pause. Pamela's grandfather sat slowly back in his chair. "That's dreadful," he said. "Terrible. How did it happen?"

"No one knows. He was found after the midday break. No one remembers seeing him go up on the hill, and no one saw him fall."

"Terrible," Pamela's grandfather said again. "I knew Henry. He was a good man."

"With a wife and three children," said Dr. Weber tightly. "I've talked to them, so you needn't bother with that."

Pamela's grandfather nodded. "Thank you, Weber. Very thoughtful. I'll see they're set right, of course."

"Money can't replace a dead husband. It can't bring back a dead father."

"Do you think I don't know that? But Henry was my employee. I have a responsibility. And his family will be extremely glad of some financial support."

"No doubt you're right." Dr. Weber took a deep breath, visibly calming himself. "I've talked to the men also. I think you should be aware that a lot of them seem to feel Henry didn't fall by accident."

"What do you mean? Wasn't it an accident?"

"Of course it was an accident. But you know how it's been all summer with the rumors and the stories. The rumor about Henry is especially persistent—the men think he saw something he wasn't supposed to see. They're very angry. I tried to calm them down, but there's been trouble brewing for a while. This may be the last straw."

"Surely you exaggerate, Weber. Rumors arise in every group of people. It hasn't struck me that they've been all that serious. I certainly haven't been aware of anything lately."

"Of course you haven't—you've been down in the crypt all day working on your infernal mosaic. You have no idea what's going on anymore."

"Now just a minute, Weber—"

"I've had enough. I don't know about the men, but this is certainly the last straw for me. I'm pulling the plug."

"Pulling . . . the . . . plug?" Pamela's grandfather repeated, as if Dr. Weber had spoken words in a foreign language.

"Yes. I am terminating the dig. I've already informed my team. The last day of excavation will be two weeks from Friday."

There was a thunderous silence. Pamela's grandfather had frozen in the act of placing his napkin beside his plate. Now, deliberately, he completed the gesture.

"I do not believe you mean that, Weber."

"I am completely serious."

"You're distressed about Henry. Sleep on it. In the morning you'll see this for the hasty and ill-considered decision it is."

"Hasty, perhaps. Ill-considered, definitely not. I've been thinking about this for weeks. I've tried to talk to you about it, but you've been too wrapped up in your damnable mosaic to listen. This dig has been one long disaster. Sickness, injury, equipment failure, morale problems, impossible working conditions—and now, a death. This is a minor site at best. We've found very little of value. I simply can't justify continuing under these conditions."

As Dr. Weber spoke, Pamela watched her grandfather's face become suffused with blood. His eyes seemed to bulge slightly.

"A minor site?" he repeated, in a tone of outrage. "Little of value?"

"That's my determination."

"How dare you?"

Dr. Weber sighed. He did not seem angry any longer, only immensely weary. "I didn't expect you to understand. I just came here to tell you. I owe you that much."

"You've overstepped yourself for the last time, Weber. I shall call Brinckerhoff tonight."

"I've already contacted my superiors. They're aware of my action, and they share my assessment of this dig. The decision has been made. There's nothing you can do about it."

Pamela had never before seen her grandfather at a loss. The blood had receded from his face. When he spoke, his voice sounded constricted.

"This is unconscionable, Weber. I don't think much of you, but I never thought you'd go behind my back."

"My only concern has been to take action as expeditiously as possible."

"I have connections, you know. I can make things very uncomfortable for you."

"I'll take my chances."

Pamela's grandfather gathered himself. His color was a little better now, but the tremor in his hands had worsened.

"Have it your way. I don't need you, or your assistants. I've bankrolled almost this entire project anyway. It can continue without you."

"It's pointless. The dig is of no value."

"The dig will remain in operation."

Dr. Weber looked at him. There was something almost like pity in his expression.

"You won't find what you're looking for, you know. It isn't there."

"I've already found what I'm looking for. The hills have been opened. The crypt has been found. The mosaic is being reconstructed. Once it's complete . . . once it's complete . . ."

He trailed off. His eyes gazed into the distance, as if something hovered there only he could see. Dr. Weber waited a moment, and then shook his head.

"I'll be going, then. I'll talk to the men tomorrow, tell them what's going to happen."

Pamela's grandfather snapped back to attention. "Kindly do no such thing. You've done enough damage. I will talk to the men."

Dr. Weber inclined his head. "As you wish." He turned toward the door and hesitated. He looked back. "I'm sorry," he said softly.

Pamela's grandfather made no reply. Dr. Weber left the room. Pamela heard his footsteps in the parlor, the closing of the front door. There was a long silence. At last her grandfather stirred.

"He is a foolish man," he said. "But it doesn't matter. He can't stop what's been started."

He was looking at Pamela. His face was abstracted and inward and somehow blind, as if he did not see her. His hooded eyes glittered, and his beaky nose jutted in his thin face. Intensity radiated from him, unhealthy somehow, as if he were being consumed from within.

He rose without saying anything more and left the room. Pamela watched him go, thin and stooped, his footsteps slow. He looked very old and very tired. She sat for a long time alone in the bright light of the dining room, putting off the moment when she must go upstairs to face the nightly struggle against sleep.

Chapter TWENTY-THREE

The next morning Pamela's grandfather went to the site, presumably to talk to the men about Dr. Weber's departure. Instead of staying all day, however, he returned early in the afternoon and shut himself in his room. He did not come down for supper, and Pamela ate in the kitchen with Esther and Sam.

Afterward she lay on her bed, staring at the ceiling. Outside a breeze stirred uneasily through the trees; it felt as if a storm was coming, though overhead the stars shone bright and unobstructed.

Abruptly there was a loud pounding at the front door. It went on and on, until Esther came from the back of the house. There was the sound of talking—Esther's low soothing tones and a man's voice, increasingly agitated. At last Esther's footsteps mounted the stairs. Pamela heard her knock at her grandfather's door.

"Sir?" she said. "Sir, Jake Whitney is here to see you. He says it's urgent." A pause. "Yes, sir, he says it's real urgent." Another pause. "All right, I'll tell him."

She descended the stairs again and said something to the man. After a moment Pamela heard the click of her grandfather's latch and his footsteps, slow and heavy. Rising, she tiptoed to her door. She opened it a little and leaned out onto the landing.

"Yes, Jake, what is it?" Pamela's grandfather was saying. "What's so important it couldn't wait till morning?"

"Sir, you have to come with me." Jake's voice was sharp and breathless. "There's a big mob of workers heading for the site. They're angry, real angry, and they mean to do damage."

"Wait a minute, Jake," Pamela's grandfather said. He sounded puzzled, as if he were half-asleep. "I don't understand you. A group of men, you say? Heading for the site?"

"It's not just a group, it's a mob! You have to help me stop them."

"But what do they intend to do at the site? Work is over for the day."

"Sir, it's not work. They're angry, angry about Henry. Now the dig's being shut down, they want what's owed them."

"The dig isn't being shut down! I told them that today."

"Yes, sir, but they know Dr. Weber is leaving, and taking all the treasure with him. He's packing it up tonight, shipping it all away."

"What's all this nonsense about treasure? There's no treasure. I thought that rumor was taken care of."

"With respect, sir, the men know it's there. They know Dr. Weber's been finding it and hiding it."

"This is preposterous!" Pamela's grandfather was angry now. "You've come here at ten o'clock at night to tell me this absurd fairy tale?"

"Sir, I know you believe what you're saying. I don't agree with the others who say you've been in on it all along—I think you've been fooled too, just like the rest of us. But we've seen them, sir, we've seen the lights on out there after it gets dark, and the people moving around on the hills. They take the treasure out at night, and hide it away so we don't see. Henry was going to prove it was there—that's why he went up on the hill. Dr. Weber and his men made up some story about him falling into the crypt by himself, but we know better. All we want's our fair share. We're entitled to it, after all we've done. Why should some people get everything, and others get nothing? This is our place. We have the right!"

"Weber's behind this," Pamela's grandfather said. "He's been trying to sabotage me all along. That's why these rumors never die down."

"You've got to believe me, sir." Jake's voice was desperate. "You have to help me. We had a meeting after work, we were going to talk about what to do, but it got out of hand. I'm telling you, they're crazy—they've got clubs, hatchets, some of them have guns. They'll wreck the place! I want my share same as anyone, but it's got to be divided up fairly, not every man for himself! If we don't stop them, no one will get anything. You have to come with me now—you're the only one who can talk to them!"

"My mosaic," Pamela's grandfather said. "They mustn't hurt my mosaic."

"It's the treasure they want, sir! We have to go now, or it will be too late! Please, sir—"

"Yes. Yes, you're right. Come, Jake. We'll go right away."

The front door slammed. There was the roar of the car engine and a crunch of gravel as it shot off into the night.

Pamela stood very still. Silence had fallen again, echoing through the house. She listened, straining her ears through the quiet, as if far away a voice had called. A breeze drifted through her open windows; the air stirred around her. It felt electric, expectant. Something is coming, Pamela thought.

Without awareness of having moved, she found herself in the hall. Below her, on the stairs, something flashed in the uncertain light. She had seen that flash before. In the stuffy house, the night dark around her, she seemed to stand beneath an open sky, from which the heavy sun poured like honey.

She descended the stairs, one by one, until she came to the place where it lay. It winked at her from the polished wood, as it had from the short grass of the hilltop: a piece of rock incised with small marching birds, tiny strutting crows. It was the fragment she had found that hot afternoon, the fragment Stern Dreamer had sent her.

Where had it come from? Could Stern Dreamer reach even into her grandfather's house? Or had her grandfather kept it, and dropped it here? But even as the questions ran through her mind she found herself stooping, her hand outstretched. This thing was hers; it had been sent to her, and she must take it. Pamela knelt. She closed her fingers around the heavy rock.

And then she knew. The waiting was over. It was time.

She got to her feet. Her body seemed light and insubstantial. She no longer felt afraid. There was only stillness, and a sense of purpose, like a call. She mounted to her room, took a light jacket from her wardrobe, and put on outdoor shoes. She ran swiftly toward the stairs.

No more than three steps down, a light sprang into existence behind her. She turned. Elizabeth, clad in the translucent silks of her negligee, stood captured in the illumination. Her long black hair hung around her shoulders. Her dark eyes were wide.

"Where are you going, Pamela?"

Pamela looked at her, silent. Elizabeth already knew the answer; Pamela could see it in her face.

"Don't go, Pamela," Elizabeth gasped. "Don't."

"I have to, Mother."

"I'll go for you. Let me face him for you."

"No, Mother." Pamela met Elizabeth's eyes. "It has to be me. It's me he's calling."

"But I've been dreaming—all these days since we saw Mirabel, ever since we came back to this terrible place. . . ."

"Oh, Mother." Pamela looked at Elizabeth. But she felt nothing. It was too late.

"I should have told you, but I'm weak. . . . I've always been weak. . . . I told myself it was only me, only me who was dreaming, because I wasn't strong enough not to believe in him. . . . I never meant it to happen this way. Please believe me, Pamela, I never meant it this way—"

"I have to go," Pamela said. Urgency was growing within her; her feet tingled with the need to move. "I'm sorry. I have to go."

"Pamela, don't!" But Pamela was already turning, running down the stairs. Behind her, she heard Elizabeth's voice, terrible with remorse: "Pamela, don't go! Pamela, come back!

I'm sorry, Pamela, I'm sorry, I'm sorry, I'm sorry—"

Pamela reached the back veranda; her mother's cries fell away. She paused briefly to take the flashlight that sat on the shelf beside the door; then, silently, she descended into the backyard and ran down the garden path, into the deep shadow of the woods.

It was almost pitch-dark. The intermittent flashes of moonlight barely penetrated the net of leaves and branches. Pamela switched on the flashlight. Its circle of brilliance danced before her, pointing the way along the path. A wind had sprung up, tossing the forest like a sea, filling the world with a great sighing, as if many voices were whispering at once. The air was chilly and damp. The rising sense of purpose was like a strong hand at her back, driving her like an arrow through the darkness.

As she neared the site, the sound of the wind was underscored with a deeper noise, gradually recognizable as distant shouting. The light was growing: a flickering, faintly ruddy brilliance. Unconsciously Pamela increased her speed. When she broke through the last rank of trees she was almost running.

She drew up short, transfixed by what lay below. The valley was on fire. The shouting came from the men who ran amid the wreckage of the dig, setting light to what was not already burning, piling tools and wood onto bonfires, smashing everything within reach. Pamela saw their faces, redly illuminated: They were twisted, maddened, mouths open in wordless cries. The roar of voices and the greedy crackle of flames were punctuated by the sound of gunshots.

Pamela was afraid now, dreadfully afraid. She knew it

would be madness to descend into that maelstrom of fire and riot, yet the purpose that had drawn her through the woods urged her forward, unrelenting, an almost physical force. She was not ready, she thought frantically. She was not strong enough. She was too afraid. Let it not be now, she implored silently. Let it be some other time, any other time, just not now. . . .

She heard a sudden stirring, all around her, like the rustling of grass or leaves. The crows, she thought, horrified, looking up. But there were no crows. The crows were gone, had been gone since that day when they all took flight. No, the rustling was something else. . . . Pamela thought she could just see burning orange eyes, moving toward her along the path. . . .

Gasping, Pamela flung herself forward. The acrid smell of smoke assaulted her nostrils; she felt the conflagration's hot breath against her body. Rivulets of flame ran along the tinder-dry grass toward the rim of the valley, tributaries to a lake of fire.

She reached the heart of the blaze, her arms flung over her head to protect her face, her eyes streaming from the choking smoke, the searing heat snatching the breath from her lungs. She dodged the shouting groups, the men running with torches or guns. Everything had fallen to the orgy of destruction. She saw the fiery remains of the long tarpaulin and the cataloging tables. The locked sheds had been pounded apart, and men had built a bonfire with the planks. Nearby blazed the broken fragments of many large wooden crates. Equipment had been overturned or smashed or set on fire. Everywhere artifacts lay scattered over the ground, ground into the dust by running feet, or charred to powder.

An overturned cart smoked up ahead; Pamela dodged around it, and suddenly the main part of the blaze was behind her. She stopped for a moment, gasping and coughing, her eyes burning so that she could scarcely see. Before her, bulking dark and solid against the sky, was the central hill. She looked up toward its summit. The purpose within her told her to climb.

Pamela set her feet on the hill's steep slope. The riot and the flames fell away below. The smell of smoke diminished and the heat faded until, as she emerged on the tablelike flatness of the hilltop, she could barely detect them. It was like entering another world. She took a deep breath, clearing her aching lungs.

There was fire here too, but it was a disciplined flicker, enclosed within a circle of people. They were very still, as if they were part of the earth. In their center a single figure knelt, hands extended over the small blaze. It was Mirabel.

Pamela moved closer. Nearly the entire Indian community was here. In the light of the little fire their faces were serene, their eyes closed. They were chanting. Mirabel led them, her body swaying, her iron gray braids swinging on either side of her face. As Pamela approached, Mirabel fell silent. She opened her eyes. One by one the others followed suit, turning their faces toward Pamela.

She stood, enclosed in the power of that unified gaze. She saw recognition in their faces, and expectancy. Very slowly Mirabel got to her feet. The others rose also. Somehow the circle had become a line, extending toward the far side of the hill. Toward the crypt.

Purpose called to Pamela without words, like a voice on the edge of hearing. It drew her toward the crypt, down into the earth, to the place where the bones of Stern Dreamer lay. She was afraid; her skin felt cold, and it was difficult to breathe. But her feet were moving, carrying her across the ravaged surface of the hilltop. She heard the chant resume behind her.

The opening of the crypt lay before her. The flagstones around it shone lighter than the earth in which they were set, and the little bird-signs were dark slashes of shadow. Far below, in the crypt itself, she could see a faint glow. Unconsciously Pamela's fingers tightened around the fragment of stone in her pocket. The top of the ladder protruded from the crypt's opening. Taking a deep breath, she swung herself onto it.

She descended, the sky, with its scattered stars, receding above her as the light below rose to meet her. All sounds disappeared, as if the outer world had dropped out of existence; Pamela heard only her own breathing, the rustling of her clothes, the soft creak as the ladder yielded to her weight.

She felt the packed earth of the floor beneath her feet and stepped back. The glow she had seen came from three lanterns, hung on posts driven into the ground. Six large tables were pushed together at the center of the crypt. They supported a vast slab, more than twelve feet along each side, flashing and glittering with mica in the soft lantern light. Her grandfather was bent over it, his hands braced on the edge of one of the tables, his head bowed, motionless.

Pamela moved forward. The carved surface of the stone unfolded itself before her. Stern Dreamer was at its center, his arms lifted, his foot raised as if engaged in some complex dance. He wore a feathered cloak and a beaked mask and a breastplate decorated with birds, and in his left hand was a long curved knife. Beneath his sandals lay a prostrate body, its chest torn open. Before him lines of tiny people knelt in reverence; behind him rose a great temple with carved pillars and doors, ranks of cloaked priests ranged along its steps. All of it—Stern Dreamer, the people, the temple—rested atop a hill, a truncated pyramid like the real hill but made of piled human skulls. Above it all, enormous wings spread and sharp claws curved to strike, hovered the image of a carrion bird. Its cruel beak and round eyes were duplicated in the features of Stern Dreamer's mask, in the carving of his breastplate. It was Crow, Stern Dreamer's totem.

There was something hypnotic about the sinuous, stylized lines of the carving, something inevitable and logical about the way they joined together to form a unified image. The mica dazzled Pamela's eyes. The breaks, where the fragments had been pieced together, were nearly invisible; it was almost as if the tablet had never been broken. It was complete, except for one small section, in the middle of Stern Dreamer's breastplate, just over his heart. There Pamela saw a gap, dark with shadow. Her eyes were drawn irresistibly toward it. A strange tingling grew in her fingers.

Her grandfather looked up. In the shifting light his face was lined and weary, shockingly old, as if years had passed since she saw him last. In his gaze Pamela saw no sign of recognition. He took a step forward.

"Give it to me," he said. His voice was like the croak of a bird.

Pamela stared at him. The tingling in her fingers was growing, and with it an almost overpowering urge to step forward and lay her hands on the tablet.

"The last piece—I must finish my work."

Pamela drew her right hand from her pocket. She looked down at her fingers, tight around the stone. The meaning of Stern Dreamer's gesture in her final dream was clear now. This had been the first piece—it was also to be the last. The tablet must be completed. Only then could Stern Dreamer wake, shaking off his long sleep and rising, fully conscious, into the world.

Pamela's grandfather saw the flash of mica. Naked, urgent desire flooded his face. "Give it to me," he whispered hoarsely. He stepped toward her, his hand extended. "Give it to me!"

Involuntarily Pamela moved back. Instead of pursuing her, her grandfather froze. A look of surprise spread over his features, tightening into a grimace of agony. His hands came up, as if to ward something off. For an instant he stood; then, heavily, he collapsed. His eyes rolled up into his head. He lay motionless.

Pamela watched him fall. It was like a film: distant, unreal. Only she and the tablet and the final piece were real; the world had narrowed until it held only these. She felt the power of the purpose that had brought her here. It was much larger than she, extending backward in time to the moment when her grandmother turned Guardianship aside and left the woods: a single moment anchoring a chain of events following inevitably one upon the other. Mirabel accepted Guardianship in her sister's place. Elizabeth in her turn rejected Guardianship. Pamela came to Flat Hills and was sent the fragment of rock, thereby setting in motion the dig, the discovery of the crypt, the reassembling of the tablet. All of it formed a pattern, a preordained design. Pamela's whole life had been a path to this moment in which she now stood, the rising power of Stern Dreamer all around her, trembling on the edge of wakefulness. For centuries he had waited. Others could dig the hill; others could reassemble the tablet. But only Pamela could set the final piece.

Pamela was at the table now, pressed against the stone; it was not cold, but warm, as if it were alive. The fingers that held the fragment ached with the need for completion. She was no longer simply herself, but the embodiment of the time Stern Dreamer had passed in sleep. When she dropped the fragment in place, those centuries would be erased. Pamela lifted her arm and extended it toward Stern Dreamer's breast.

Poised on the edge of completion, Pamela hesitated. It seemed that she could hear something . . . a voice, rising and falling in a low, repetitive chant. Something in it held her, even as the tide of Stern Dreamer's power strove to sweep her away. There were words in the chant, words Pamela could not quite make out. They vibrated softly beneath the compulsion that burned in her fingers, widening the narrowed pinpoint of her consciousness, reaching into her mind, empty a moment ago of anything except Stern Dreamer's purpose.

Something struggled inside Pamela, something at her core, straining against the force that held her. There was a familiar quality to that voice, to its cadences and rhythms. Pamela recognized it at last: It was Mirabel. Mirabel was calling to her, trying to tell her something important. In her mind images grew. She saw the sun on the floor of a cottage in the woods, hanks of yarn bubbling in blue dye, a path where goldenseal grew, a group of children listening wide-eyed to a legend. The pictures came to her like individual drops of water falling into a still pool, joining to become a trickle, then a flood. They linked, became a whole, a chain of memory.

Where she had seen only one path, Pamela now saw two. In the first, Stern Dreamer's power drew her to the hills, toward the moment of completion. In the second, Mirabel's wisdom guided her through the forest, among the legends of her heritage, toward the task of Guardianship. The paths lay together; she had been walking both of them at once. They led to this moment, to her trembling hand above the dark space in the glittering stone tablet. But from their convergence followed their separation. This moment was more than a moment of completion. It was a moment of choice.

The chant wound around Pamela like a cleansing wind, filling her mind with light. The inexorability she had seemed to see only an instant ago was an illusion. Nothing was inevitable—not her grandmother's actions, not Elizabeth's, not her own. It had been choice that shaped their lives, just as it had been Stern Dreamer's choice to take Crow as totem, just as it had been Willow Withe's choice to accept Cougar and reject what her father offered. Now it was Pamela's turn. She could complete the tablet, or she could leave it unfinished. She could surrender to Stern Dreamer's power, or she could resist. In the end, Stern Dreamer could not wake unless she chose to awaken him.

Pamela realized that her fingers were no longer tingling. The overpowering compulsion was gone. Slowly she lowered her arm to her side. The world around her expanded as the hold of Stern Dreamer's power fell away. She felt its strength receding, dying back into centuries, shrinking like a candle flame in a pool of wax. There was a finality to it, like the closing of a door that had been open too long. At last even the tiniest spark of power was gone. Stern Dreamer slept once more.

Chapter TWENTY-FOUR

For a moment Pamela stood dazed, as if waking from a long dream. She could no longer hear the chant. The crypt was just a room now, the tablet just a carved slab of stone. A little distance away she saw her grandfather. He was lying as he had fallen. Only the faintest motion of his chest showed that he was still alive.

All the concern she had not felt earlier propelled Pamela to his side. She knelt and felt his forehead: It was cold. The flesh of his face was slack and gray. His labored breath rasped.

Quickly she climbed the ladder, the lantern light sinking away beneath her. As she emerged onto the hilltop she saw the Indians, standing as she had left them. They came to meet her. Two of the men began to descend into the crypt. The others gathered around her, their faces weary yet elated. Among them she saw Seth.

Mirabel came forward and took Pamela's hands. She was smiling, and her face was filled with joy.

"My grandfather—," Pamela began. Mirabel nodded.

"He served Stern Dreamer, but not of his own will. We will take care of him." Mirabel raised her palm and placed it against Pamela's cheek. "You have done well, Pamela. Stern Dreamer sleeps."

"Is he gone forever?"

"No. He cannot be gone forever. But the line of succession has been restored. The breach has been healed. He sleeps. He will continue to sleep as long as you are Guardian, and your daughters after you." Mirabel nodded gravely. "Yes, Pamela. You are Guardian now. Down there in the crypt, you fought your battle, and you won."

"Guardian," Pamela repeated. The word felt strange on her tongue. She had seen the two paths before her as she stood pressed against Stern Dreamer's tablet, but the reality of what she had done came home to her now. She shook her head.

"It was you, Mirabel. Your chant. If I hadn't heard it . . . I nearly completed the tablet, you know."

"I know. But I only helped you, as I promised I would. It was you who made the final decision."

"How can I be Guardian?" Pamela entreated her. "I don't know enough. I'm not strong enough. You're the Guardian, Mirabel. You're the one who knows everything. You're the one who's strong."

"Pamela." Mirabel smiled into Pamela's face, and her smile was like the rising sun. "I'll be by your side for as long as you want me. I'll guide and train and support you, as the women of our tribe have always done. But you are Guardian, like it or not. The task has passed from me. This is your path now. You chose it."

"I'm afraid," Pamela whispered.

"I know. It's a great burden to be Guardian of Stern Dreamer's sleep." Mirabel gripped Pamela's hands tightly. "This is what you were meant for, Pamela. Listen to your blood—your Indian blood. It will always show you how to go."

Pamela pulled away from Mirabel and moved toward the edge of the hill. Her fear was like a weight on her chest. The path before her, so natural in the crypt, now loomed like a mountain, fraught with difficulties and overwhelming responsibility. She knew she had chosen, as Mirabel said—she could remember the moment of choice, could still feel Stern Dreamer's power as it began to slip away. Yet she struggled against what she saw before her. Until the last few months she had lived her life in complete ignorance of her lineage. How could she commit herself to a life and a people she had known for so short a time? How could she give up the life she had always expected to have? She was not of this world. She was barely even of this race. The burden was too great.

For the first time, she became aware that the riot below had ceased. The fire had burned itself out at its center, though it was still alive at the edges, licking along the dry grass toward the forest. Among the ashes the rioters milled aimlessly, as if their purpose had disappeared. They seemed bewildered, like men waking from a dream. Some supported each other away from the site, toward the road; some stood in ragged groups; others sat amid the wreckage, their hands loose and empty.

Far off across the width of the valley, Pamela thought she saw something stirring in the shadows. It took shape as she watched, moving across the ground in great leaping strides. It was among the flames now; sparks flashed from tawny fur, from sinuous muscles and a round blunt head. The creature parted the listless men like water; it mounted the steep hillside in effortless bounds. Cresting the top of the hill, it came to a stop a little distance away. Its face was turned to Pamela's, its round eyes orange with the reflection of the lingering flames below. It was impossible, yet completely, solidly real: the creature of Pamela's dreams, the great cat she had seen on her grandfather's lawn, the totem of the legend. Cougar.

Pamela felt her heart beating. Her pulse seemed to resonate throughout her body, shaking her to her fingertips. Hardly aware of what she was doing, she moved toward the beast. She could see its great sides, heaving with the exertion of its run, its long whiskers, its sharp claws, its powerful hindquarters. Unblinking, its luminous eyes met hers. In them was recognition. It had come for her, as it had come for Willow Withe and all the women of her line. Slowly she lifted her hand and extended it toward Cougar's head. Softly she placed her fingers against its fur.

For an instant Pamela felt the living creature beneath her touch: the rough coat, the heavy bones, the warmth of life, an answering pulse that matched her own. For a moment, as their hearts beat together, Pamela sensed the blood of which Mirabel had spoken. It filled her like the rush of a subterranean river, separate and darkly alive, unknown and powerful. It was part of her whether she wished it or not. Whether she wished it or not, it would lead her from now on. She had chosen the path she would follow, but the blood could not be chosen. It simply was.

Pamela was still afraid. Yet within her fear she saw the possibility of understanding. She would learn. She would grow. She would endure. And someday she would pass the burden on. She saw the line of her descendants stretching out before her; behind her marched the procession of her ancestors. She was the link that bound them together, making them a chain to hold what must be held in this place. This was her world: the valley of the hills.

Beneath her hand, the cat grew insubstantial. As she watched, it flickered, fading at last from view. Her hand rested on empty air. Slowly she raised it to her cheek. She could still feel Cougar's warmth; it seemed that a trace of cat scent clung to her fingers.

Pamela turned back to the others. They stood a little distance away in a rough semicircle, Mirabel a little in front. She wore that expression of joy again; behind her, the others' faces were grave with reverence. Pamela saw Seth, watching her with awe, as if she were a ghost. But she was not a ghost, or even a Guardian now: She was just an exhausted girl, trembling with a weariness she had not realized till this moment. She stared at the faces before her, frightened at what she saw there.

After a long moment Seth moved; he came to stand before her. He held out his hand. She placed hers in it. Their fingers linked.

Pamela felt something wet on her cheek—tears? But another drop came, and another. A gentle rain was falling, soaking her clothes and hair. Below, in the wrecked valley, the grass fires were dying in a welter of hissing steam. Still the rain fell, harder and harder, from a sky the dark color of lead; it washed over the parched and ravaged earth, healer of wounds, bringer of life, the final seal on the closing of a terrible door. Pamela raised her face and let the water wash the soot and dust from her skin. She felt Seth's hand in hers, warm and strong and steady. It was, somehow, like the completion of all her choices.

Epilogue

Rapidly now, Pamela's mind rose up through layers of memory, toward the present day.

They had gone home through the wet forest, Pamela and Seth hand in hand, Mirabel at their side, behind them two men bearing a stretcher on which Pamela's grandfather lay. In the house, Elizabeth was waiting, pale and quiet. Her dark eyes were fearful, but at least she had not retreated again into distance. She went off with her father to the hospital without a word.

Pamela's grandfather had suffered a stroke. When he returned from the hospital he was unable to speak, and the right side of his body was paralyzed. He spent his days in a wheelchair in the parlor, or on the porch if the weather was mild, a gaunt, frail ghost of himself. Often Pamela sat with him. Looking in his eyes, she sensed that his mind was clear; she could only imagine how terrible it must be for him to exist like this, caged within his own body. Did he realize what he had almost done? she wondered. Did he understand the power that had filled him? Did he know that by attempting to eradicate the legends he had in fact fulfilled them? He died six months later, without ever regaining the power of speech. But Pamela thought she knew the answers.

Gradually Elizabeth returned to life. She took over her

father's business concerns, she ran the household, she became more social and less withdrawn. But she was not the person she had been. She never fully regained her vitality. There was a slowness in her that had not been there before, as if something essential had been taken away. She still sat for long hours in her room; as the years passed she lost her beauty, growing very fat. She never spoke of the events of that summer, and she never discussed with Pamela the choice Pamela had made. The subject of Guardianship was a blank between them, a thing that was accepted but could never be mentioned.

Dr. Weber and his men left the day after the riot, taking nothing with them, for there was nothing left to salvage. The people of Flat Hills tried to put what had happened behind them. The riot had been like a terrible vision, a moment out of time; in the gray light of morning, it was difficult to believe it had not been a dream. The townspeople gratefully took up their normal lives, and soon Flat Hills was just as it had been. But it was never quite forgotten that a great treasure had once been within reach, before it was stolen away.

Pamela returned to the valley a few days after the fire. The rain had persisted without a break since that night; beneath a heavy sky the wreckage of the dig lay black and hideous, a morass of mud and ash. But groups of Indians, under Mirabel's direction, had already begun to clean it up. They had hauled away much of the debris, smoothed out the ruts and gouges, and reburied the shattered artifacts. Mirabel herself had descended to the crypt and destroyed Stern Dreamer's tablet a second time, pounding the shards into powder. She had replaced the flagstones and sealed the crypt once more.

The hills were rebuilt. Pamela labored with the others,

gathering earth in baskets, turning it out, tramping it down to make a new surface. It was hard work, but joyous: There was singing, and everyone laughed and joked. Eventually the hills lay restored, flat and unmarked as ever. The valley was clean. It only remained for spring to do its work, for the silver grass to grow again. Then, at last, Stern Dreamer's tomb would be fully closed.

In the years that followed, Pamela led a double life. There was her school life—though still outcast, she nevertheless managed to gain an uneasy tolerance among her classmates—and there was her life in the woods, in which Mirabel continued the task of training her to fulfill her Guardianship. It was difficult, exacting work; sometimes Pamela despaired of ever getting it right. Yet that night on the hill, when she looked Cougar in the eyes, she had reached the place within her where Willow Withe dwelled. When things grew overwhelming, she could reach down to that part of herself and borrow a little of her ancestor's strength.

When the time came, Pamela went away to college. Mirabel and Pamela had agreed that one of Pamela's tasks would be to guide the villagers into the modern world; to this end, she needed a modern education. From college she went on to law school. In the summers she continued to learn from Mirabel.

After seven long years spent mostly elsewhere, Pamela had returned to Flat Hills for good. Now, at last, she would begin her Guardianship in earnest.

Pamela opened her eyes. The sun flooded the valley with light, and the short silver grass glowed like the pelt of an animal. Once again, the ghosts of the past were laid; her fear was gone. She felt nothing now but peace.

She got to her feet and descended the slope. She walked across the uneven ground, toward the forest. She was not surprised to see that someone was waiting for her, just inside the first fringe of trees.

"Seth," she said. She went toward him; his arms reached out for her. She felt the warmth of his body, smelled the clean pine scent of his hair. After a moment he held her away from him.

"How did you know I was here?"

He smiled. "I always know."

"I'm back for good now."

He nodded. He himself had returned several years ago. He had got the education he wanted, through a route no one would have predicted: He had joined the army. He attended college on the G.I. Bill and was now going to medical school; once he was finished, he planned to open his own practice.

Seth too had been changed by that night on the hill. It had not been easy for him to give up his long fight to conquer the legends within himself, but what he had seen could not be rejected. He had come at last to understand the importance of Pamela's choice, and his part in it. He was still determined to live in the modern world, and to bring change to his people, but he no longer wanted to leave Flat Hills.

"I've been remembering," Pamela said.

Seth's face changed fractionally; he let go of her. She stepped away, frowning a little.

"Seth, will you always be afraid of me?"

He looked at her. "I don't know."

"I hate it when you look at me like that. The way they all used to look at Mirabel. As if I wasn't a person. As if I was a . . . a spirit."

"I'm sorry, Pamela." He dropped his eyes. "I don't feel that way most of the time. But I can never quite forget you're the Guardian. None of us can. It's the way it must be."

The valley seemed darker now, as if a shadow had passed across the sun. The peace had receded a little, and Pamela felt within her the faint, cold consciousness of what lived in the hills. She sighed, feeling reality and its burdens close around her. Seth was right, she thought to herself. It had to be that way.

But sun still flooded through the trees, and Seth's presence was warm beside her; in Mirabel's cabin waited honey-sweetened corn cakes and cool sumac drink.

"Come on, Seth," she said. She linked her arm with his, and smiled up into his face. "Let's go tell Mirabel I'm home."

Close together, they walked into the woods. The trees closed around them, shutting the valley from view. Behind them, silent and empty, the hills basked in the sun. The hills slept. But dimly, at their heart, consciousness endured. It had waited for centuries, for eons; it could wait eons more if it had to, for the time to come again. One day, the binding power was bound to loosen. One day, a Guardian would fail her test. And then, Crow would return. Light would rest again on smooth black flagstones. And the waking, at last, could begin.

About This Book

Guardian of the Hills is a work of fiction. The town of Flat Hills, the valley, the tribe of Native Americans living in the forest—all are the product of my imagination. They are based, however, on solid historical fact.

There really is a Quapaw Indian tribe, located in Arkansas as well as in other southern states. I have taken the liberty of inventing my own small branch of it for the purposes of this novel.

There really was a Mound Culture (more accurately known as the Mississippian Culture). It emerged about A.D. 800 and reached its height between A.D. 1200 and 1500. Its people—ancestors of the present-day Cherokee, Choctaw, Seminole, and other southern Native American tribes—built elaborate ceremonial centers, featuring massive earthworks, all across the southeastern United States, from Georgia to as far west as Oklahoma, and from Florida to as far north as Illinois. Among the largest are Moundville in Alabama, Etowah in Georgia, Spiro in Oklahoma, and Cahokia in Illinois. The structure of the religion practiced among the mounds is not fully known; but its mysterious symbols, known as the Southeastern Ceremonial Complex, are well documented by archaeology.

Most of the great Mississippian ceremonial centers were abandoned by the mid-1500s, and the Mississippian Culture itself was gone by the mid-1700s. Many modern scholars believe that the culture's decline may have been initiated by the ill-fated 1539 expedition of Hernando de Soto, with its introduction of European diseases.

Mississippian mounds fascinate all who encounter them. Unfortunately, the prejudices of the earliest observers fostered the belief that Native Americans could not possibly have built such elaborate structures and resulted in strange theories of a superior race of "Mound Builders," who were believed to be anything from a lost tribe of Israel to giant Vikings. It was not until the late nineteenth century that these myths were finally laid to rest, and Native Americans at last received their due.

For those interested in finding out more about the Mississippian Culture, a good general source is *Prehistory of North America*, by Jesse D. Jennings (McGraw-Hill, 1974). For an interesting account of Mound Builder theories, see *Mound Builders of Ancient America: The Archaeology of a Myth*, by Robert Silverberg (New York Graphic Society, 1968). Charles Hudson is an authority on prehistoric Native American societies in the Southeast; his *Elements of Southeastern Indian Religion* (E. J. Brill, 1984) and *The Southeastern Indians* (University of Tennessee Press, 1976) are extremely informative.